CW00504517

The Soul Feaster

By Philip Lyndon

The Soul Feaster

"For every thousand hacking at the leaves of evil there is one striking at the root..." Thoreau.

Alzarin Crimson

The sound tore through her ears, a hollow visceral screech like that of a skewered monstrous bird. Through eyes muddied with rivulets of her own blood Kate Sinclair fought in vain to protect herself from the frenzied clawing. Crashing from wall to wall within her luxury apartment, the attack on Kate was relentless.

The sable hairs of the paintbrush splayed, oozing Alzarin Crimson, pressure forcing the pigment into the pores of the rough canvas. Kessler was energised; his brush danced across the painting, white consumed by red.

Colliding against the living room wall, the rapid blood loss ebbing her energy, like an over wound automaton Kate thrashed her arms in futile defence. As her veins drained so too did any hope of escape.

Sombre black now added an inky darkness to the reds. Coarse fibres scored through the thick paint, Kessler's brush moving in virtuoso flourishes.

As her life was stolen Kate made one last gesture, pressing her bloodied hand against the stark white of the wall she made the sign of the cross.

Scarlet Lake

Detective Inspector Leighton stared down at Kate Sinclair's mutilated body.

"Ironic... don't you think? To see a *Solicitor* bled dry?" Having been through an acrimonious divorce with the legal profession having desolated his finances he felt vindicated to comment.

The Scenes of Crime Officer offered up no reply, continuing to record photographs of the body. Meanwhile Detective Sergeant Joseph was absorbed by the bloodied cross on the wall.

"Alright, alright," said Leighton, waving the photographer aside, "you're not shooting a bloody Vogue cover. Out the way- let the dog see the rabbit."

The photographer rolled his eyes in retreat.

Leighton squatted down beside the corpse, his knees cracking. He glanced at his sergeant, "Why so quiet?"

Joseph's gaze was still fixed on the smear of blood that formed the rudimentary cross. He had been somehow reminded of the police report on his parents' violent deaths twenty years ago. Naturally as a child he had been unable to deal with events, but later, as a Police Officer, had come detachment and he had revisited that report, studied it, word by word, always concluding its explanations flawed. That cross on the wall... strangely there were echoes.

"Joseph?" Leighton fished, "What you make of that?"

"Was she religious?" Joseph questioned, "Do we know?"

Leighton snorted, "Un-bloody likely. Ms. Sinclair was a cold, ruthless, bitch... no disrespect to the dead. Money, status and Power were her holy trinity. High flying Solicitor with a who's who of wealthy clientele. If the price was right she'd represent the Devil himself. I've come up against Ms. Sinclair before .... I'm talking in court... not in the biblical sense," his unruly eyebrows danced. Leighton gestured round the room, "Look at it..... Every luxury... even original art dripping off the walls."

"Well if she wasn't religious in life," Joseph remarked, "Maybe facing death she reconsidered?"

They turned their attention back to Sinclair's body, slumped against the wall; her once smart suit slashed and stained dark, eyes wide, one false eyelash askew like a frazzled caterpillar.

As Dave Joseph looked at her, he was again reminded of his parents' deaths - animalistic and brutal. The thought twisted his gut…… *Detach…. detach.*

"What- a- carve up!" Leighton's voice pulled Joseph back.

"What we got to go on Guv?"

Leighton stretched and rolled his shoulders, "Not a bloody lot! A sustained savage attack, a smashed bathroom window entry / exit point. Looks like we pin all hopes on the crime scene boys and let them work some magic…. see what they turn up….. Whoopee-fucking-do!"

"And a motive? Nothing taken ….?" said Joseph, scanning the room's art work. "The paintings Guv, some displaced but….hang fire….. look at *that* one…. it's what…*Melted*?"

Joseph drew closer to the canvas and studied it. The surface was darkened, pitted, red and molten in places. He leaned in closer; there was a residual odour….. like that of spent matches or a child's cap gun. Little of the original image remained, but in the bottom right hand corner he could just discern a signature,

Tybalt Kessler.

Cerulean Blue

With her dark gypsy hair pulled back behind her ears, violet eyes refusing to blink, Sam Paris bit at her bottom lip, concentrating on holding the brush steady. Standing in front of her easel in the kitchen/diner Sam held her breath, like a sniper readying to pull the trigger, exhaling only as she completed the tiny painted detail. The picture had to be finished in time.

The sound of the front door opening broke her concentration; she glanced at her watch- 6:30pm!

"I come bearing gifts," Dave Joseph held aloft a brown paper bag wafting curry aroma in Sam's direction. He kissed her on the cheek, "How's the masterpiece coming along?"

"Great! Nearly there!" Sam set to work cleaning her brushes.

Dave had picked up her mobile phone from the kitchen counter. "One missed call Missus! That's me... telling you I'll pick up dinner."

"I had no idea I'd worked so late... guess I was in *the zone*; time is a thief and all that. Anyway, how was your day?"

"Eventful!" said Dave, upturning the foil containers with the delicacy of a bricklayer. "As we're about to eat I'll spare you the gruesome details but actually I need to pick your brains. At the crime scene today we found a painting, looked like it had been burned... Melted? I don't know.... and it had this smell...like... gunpowder to it...really weird, no idea how it got that way. Anyway it was by Tybalt Kessler. I've heard you mention him.... see I do listen to you when you get all arty farty..." he smirked, "and I'd like to know more. What's the score with him?"

Sam flicked the tea towel at Dave's rear, "Cheeky bugger!"

They carried the plates to the table and sat down.

Sam continued," Well if indeed you were truly listening...... you'd know he has links to the University?"

said Sam, "He funded the Art wing, judges our end of year exhibition. What else? He lives in France but also has a studio here in Old Portsmouth... in one of the old warehouses. Who is lucky enough to have one of his paintings? They go for a bomb! He has quite a reputation."

"The owners not so lucky- she's dead! What kind of reputation?" asked Dave through a mouthful of Chicken Tikka Masalla.

"Oh....Ah well, there are those who say his paintings have an *aura* about them. Kessler explains it by saying that paintings *choose their owners*. Of course it could all be just great PR but he certainly commands a high price. Helpful?"

"Hmm yeah.. Intriguing," said Dave crunching popadom with his curry, "I'm starving, been on the go all day with only a limp panini for lunch."

"Slow down Gutty! You'll get heartburn," Sam rapped his knuckles with her fork. "Hey you should speak to Professor Naismith about Kessler" said Sam.

"Your tutor?"

"Yes, he's the art guru..... and he organises the exhibition, oh and don't forget you'll see Kessler for yourself exhibition night. That's if I ever get my painting finished!

Brown Madder

Doctor Lesley Terry handed the post mortem report to D.I. Leighton.

"I thought I'd hand it over in person." she said, "I can anticipate your reaction when you read it and want to reassure you I haven't flipped my lid!"

Dave Joseph watched as Leighton read, he could tell by the D.I.'s expression that the findings would worsen the Guv's already poor mood.

"What the bloody hell? Due respect and all doctor, but this makes no bloody sense. You been around those corpses and chemicals too long." He tossed the report to Joseph who scanned through it quickly. He understood Leighton's reaction. The report made especially grim reading

....*multiple wounds exposing muscle and bone suggesting sustained attack by large clawed animal. Pattern of wounds shows two sets of three claws. Swabs taken show trace deposits of sulphurous matter.* Joseph skipped to the last page ....*cause of death exsanguination.*

Doctor Terry shook her head, "The wounds are more in keeping with an attack by a large animal on the plains of Africa, although how something like that got to the fourth floor is your problem, oh, and by the way the sulphurous matter in the wounds is also present on swabs taken from the broken bathroom window."

Dave scanned more of the report, "This is weird shit...." he muttered.

"Think we all agree there," said Leighton.

With Leighton tied up with a court appearance, Dave had their shared office to himself. The PM report on Kate Sinclair had thrown up more questions than it answered. The time of death was consistent with witness reports of a noisy disturbance around 3:00am. What caused that disturbance and killed Kate Sinclair was a mystery other than it had claws, could enter through a fourth floor window, and seemed to toy with its victim as a cat might with a mouse.

Dave pushed the file to one side, took a glug of coffee from the Styrofoam cup on his desk and turned his attention to the PC screen. The analysis of the Kessler painting was still in progress and Dave could not shift it from his mind. Sam had fascinated him further with talk of auras associated with works by the artist.

"Let's find out more about you .....*Kessler*." Dave typed the name into the search engine and watched the hits appear. He opened the artist's official site and studied each section, learning the artist had been born in Sweden, his parents both teachers he a gifted child. His subsequent success had him living mostly in a 15th century chateau in the Dordogne attached to a vast vineyard. He had set up *The Kessler Foundation*, a charitable concern into which considerable profits from the sale of his art work were channelled to benefit worthy causes worldwide. As Sam had mentioned Kessler owned a studio in Old Portsmouth preferring to live in the naval city, rather than the capital, when he was in the UK. He had formed a strong link with the University and funded a state of the art wing dedicated to the development of new artistic talent. Starting last year he had appeared end of summer term to judge and award the Kessler Gold Prize, choosing the student's work he most favoured.

Dave leaned back and smiled as he thought of how excited Sam was on nearing completion of her picture for the exhibition. He didn't profess to know much about art but he loved her study of clear water lapping over smooth round pebbles.

The only section of the website left for Dave to explore was that of examples of Kessler's work. He clicked on the thumbnail and as it uploaded onto the screen he felt an inexplicable sensation run through him, a mixture akin to dread and excitement combined with a flash of heat like that sudden blast of an oven door being opened. He reached for his coffee and his shaking hand sent it spilling from the cup.

"SHIT, SHIT, SHIT." lifting his keyboard from the

advancing liquid Dave called to the outer office, "SOMEONE, GET PAPER TOWELS, PLEASE?"

Renaissance Gold

Professor Charles Naismith's voice boomed across the lecture theatre.

"The birth of Art lies in the crude cave paintings of our ancestors."

Students gawped at images on the giant plasma screen; ancient animals depicted in earthy tones.

"In early representations the subject matter was often that of an animal hunted for survival".

Dave glanced at his Tissot watch, a valued birthday gift from Sam, as he crossed the University car park. He had decided to take Sam's suggestion, arranging to meet with the *art guru* Naismith. He wasn't really sure why but the case had stalled and Kessler and his work had sparked the detective's curiosity.

Surfing the internet in the last few days, Dave had found there were some remarkable incidents connected to Kessler's works:

A wealthy industrialist had perished, his factory razed to the ground, a painting by Kessler in the boardroom had mysteriously survived intact. The diametric opposite of what had happened in the Sinclair case.

A fashion designer known only as *Mantois* had been savagely murdered, the crime attributed, depending on which tabloid one read, to a crazed fan or jilted lover. At the designers home his Kessler original had been obliterated with scrawled illegible writing in the designers own blood.

Then there was the picture donated by Kessler himself to a Romanian orphanage. Known to locals as *Salvation* it had attracted worldwide attention, celebrity visits and huge donations transforming the fortunes of many children.

The paradox was enthralling.

Each time Dave had viewed Kessler's work online he had felt a strong response, it was as if the art cut through barriers and communicated direct to his core. Feeling exposed in this way was something he tried to avoid in all aspects of his life but he had to admit the hints of liberation that came with it had a seductive draw.

Reaching reception Dave signed in and was duly given directions to the lecture theatre. Walking there he glanced, largely unimpressed, at the numerous examples of students' work seemingly hanging on every wall; then one stopped him in his tracks.....

A large charcoal sketch of a young man dressed in a hoodie and torn jeans, hanging on a towering steel cross. A card underneath it read:

Contemporary Crucifixion by Liz Freeman - Winner Kessler Gold Prize.

Dave gasped for breath; images flashed across his mind...the blood smear cross at Sinclair's flat....his mother's hand tightly clutching her own silver crucifix, his father lying dead beside her in their shared blood...

Dave felt his stomach lurch and ducked into the nearby toilets. He let the cold water run into the sink and wetting some paper towels he soaked his face. The loss of composure was out of character, what had got into him?

"The earliest religions- Shamanism, Paganism- emphasised animals, the natural world, elemental forces."

Naismith adjusted his glasses on their gold chain as he glanced at his notes.

"Arts real development ran parallel with the evolution of religion. Organised religion brought moving imagery, potent in meaning...."

Dave slipped into a seat at the back of the lecture theatre; he was early despite his stop off at the gents.

Naismith was in full flow, as he spoke vibrant images of religious masterpieces filled the screen. "Churches stood, beacons to mans faith, towering heavenward; transmitters of worship. Stained glass fired emotions with its jewelled hues....."

Dave stifled a yawn.

"Much of mans thought was preoccupied with gratitude to his God, reverence to his Saints and denouncement of the Devil."

Dave felt his eyelids leaden and Naismith's voice become a drone, he fought the urge to doze and tuned back in to hear Naismith's finale.

"One could say these artists... these craftsmen.... truly experienced.....Divine Inspiration."

The lights came up in the theatre and the shuffling of feet as students rose from their seats prompted Dave to move; he made his way to stage.

"Professor Naismith? Detective Sgt. Dave Joseph." he extended his hand," Thanks for seeing me."

"Quite alright Detective," Naismith's glasses fell on their gilt chain as he gathered up his notes. "As you can see things get quieter once all the bright young things filter from Establishment, so I have a window!"

"Sam mentioned you would be a good source of information on Kessler. He isn't under investigation himself, I'm interested in incidents involving some of his paintings."

"Ah," Naismith's eyes glinted, "The *Kessler curse!*" he paused then let out a deep belly laugh," Utter balderdash of course. From what I know the few deaths, somewhat tenuously, associated with his paintings are those of wealthy, ambitious, egotistical and unscrupulous individuals. Success, power and fame bring all the associated trappings, including resentment and undesirable attention. We are, Detective a world of *haves* and *have nots* and the latter often like to shake the former from their lofty perches!"

Dave felt as though he could fall victim to another lecture but had to agree the professor was right, all the victims lived lives with the potential to attract enemies borne of envy, and bitter enemies can hatch vengeful retribution.

"It's the way they died that's of interest to me, especially the anomalies at the crime scenes though I agree in each instance there was no lack of motive."

Naismith stuffed his collected notes into a soft leather case then tucked it under his arm," Well I'm happy to assist you with whatever conundrums you may have. It's all rather thrilling! Shall we retreat to my office?"

"Thank you. In truth I'm not sure what I say will make a lot of sense, but I would ask you to treat it in the strictest confidence?"

"Of course Dear boy, please speak freely," said the professor as he marched across the stage to the exit door.

Organised chaos was the only way to describe Naismith's office.

On entering the professor flung his case on top of a filing cabinet and slumped into a huge high backed leather chair. His desk looked like a still life study his students might sketch, scattered with files, print outs, at least three visible half drunk coffee mugs and an old apple core standing, stalk up, beside an ivory coloured phone in the need of a wipe. The bookcases behind groaned under the weight of art and historical reference books.

"Can I offer you tea? Coffee?" the professor wildly gestured to a tray and kettle perched precariously on another of the filing cabinets "Frothy coffee with chocolate sprinkles?"

"No thanks; I'm fine." Dave didn't want to attract yet more anarchy to the scene.

"You'll excuse me if I sift as we talk? I'm perfectly adept at multitasking." Naismith licked his thumb and flicked through some papers starting yet another pile to join its towering counterparts. He squinted before pulling his spectacles up and perching them on his nose, "I agree the deaths are all very peculiar. A marked amount of symbolism present, most fascinating."

On their way from the lecture theatre Dave had shared details of the various cases but had omitted mention of his parents' deaths. There was, after all, no Kessler connection, yet why did he still feel it relevant? The verdict of the inquest had been murder/suicide. True his father had undergone a dramatic personality change in the months before; losing his job, becoming aggressive, withdrawn, depressed. But as with the Kessler cases there were puzzling anomalies. A knife found between the bodies could not satisfactorily explain the nature of the numerous wounds found on his parents, and suicide…? Who uses the *death of a thousand cuts* as their method -however tortured their mind?

"The fashion designer fellow, what was his name?" Naismith's voice jolted Dave back to the present, "French sounding chap, remind me?"

"Mantois." said Dave.

"You said Mantois' blood formed the text on the painting?"

"Yes, it was matched"

"I wonder….. post or ante mortem? Did he witness the act? I shudder at the thought."

"Good point. It was assumed after death, it was a bloodbath at the scene."

"And what…" asked Naismith, drawing in the air with his index finger, "…did the perpetrator use to write with? A digit? Were there fingerprints?"

Dave shook his head, "Actually… it was more like the nib of a pen… so no prints." He felt tempted to add, *Sherlock*. He liked how the professor's mind worked, despite the physical chaos there was organised thought.

"I'd like to see this writing, if it is permissible?"

"I can't see why not, it's a cold case and if it helps in the current investigation… I'll pull some strings, see what I can do."

"Ah yes, the death of the Solicitor." Naismith closed in hands in front of his chin, his elbows on the armrests of his leather chair." I'll bet she had some enemies?"

"More than first thought." Dave paused, "I have to remind you again this is all confidential."

Naismith closed his eyes for a moment in acknowledgement.

Dave continued, "Looking into her affairs, it's been established that she was instrumental in several miscarriages of justice. Put simply a number of seriously pissed off individuals found themselves behind bars-sacrificial lambs, doing time in place of others higher up the food chain."

"As all through history; the pawns fall before the King," Naismith sighed, gesturing to the books behind him, "Another passion."

"Art and history." said Dave, "Your lecture went down well."

"Thank you. Religious art... a broad subject. Difficult for the bright young things to appreciate the power it once had. We live in an age now where we are bombarded with imagery- selling us everything from cars to bras!"

Dave laughed.

"We are saturated with imagery these days; we even have cameras in our bless*ed* phones." Naismith continued, "Some tribal cultures still believe the camera steals the soul. Ha...I think they have a point! Nowadays their indignity would be furthered by having their *soul* posted on some wretched *social networking* site for inaccurately labelled *friends* to pass comment on!"

"Not a fan I take it professor?" Dave knew himself guilty of the crime.

"Excuse my rant! There was some point....what was it? Ah yes," Naismith held up one of his print outs. "Before the dawn of photography, before TV, its ribald cousin, insatiable at one end incontinent at the other, images meant something to us, Art moved us, astounded us, Art spoke to our souls."

Dave's face paled, recalling the way he felt viewing at Kessler's work. He looked at the print held before him.

Naismith announced, "*The Temptation of St Anthony by Mathis Grunewald* circa 1512. Part of the Seinheim altar piece," he spoke as though Dave might be familiar with the information.

Dave gave a nod.

The Professor continued, "Grunewald ranks as one of the

finest German painters of the Renaissance, his speciality-emotive religious scenes- brutal, vibrant."

Dave feared another lengthy lecture.

"The altar piece stood in the chapel of an Abbey caring for plague victims in the hope its subject matter, St. Anthony, may affect a miracle or offer some comfort."

Dave brought to mind the Kessler *Salvation* painting in the Romanian orphanage.

He studied the Grunewald- In it monstrous creatures attacked the elderly white bearded St Anthony dragging him by his hair.

Naismith smiled as he watched Dave." On first viewing one wouldn't be aware its theme is actually one of healing? See there, bottom right of the picture....... that painted scrap of paper with text? The translation reveals its plea, *Jesus where were you? Why did you not help me and heal my wounds?*

The image momentarily morphed: Dave saw again the smudged cross on Sinclair's wall... the small bright silver cross around his mother's neck, her hand clutching it in death as a drowning man might cling to a vessel's wreckage. Dave blinked; the image of St Anthony returned. The Saint seemed to be clutching rosary beads, a riot of grotesques surrounding him. At this moment of grave peril..... He *too* turned to the cross. Sweat broke out on Dave's back; this he thought was the true meaning of terror.

Naismith, noting the expression on Dave's face, congratulated himself at having made his point so effectively. His voice piped in jubilation, "Fear not! There in the sky...." he pointed to a swirling cloud above the fearful scene. "Christ responding to the Saints plea is despatching his angels to combat Satan's demons."

Naismith placed the sheet of paper on his desk, "So you see, Art can be provocative, powerful. In a sense it has energy, the artist's mood, and the viewers' response- strong emotions transmitted, received. Telepathy of sorts. A communication that can transcend even time."

Dave was acutely aware of this powerful energy. He needed little reminder. He wondered if he dare confide in Professor Naismith the emotive response he was experiencing.

"Interestingly Tybalt Kessler's work shares some elements with Grunewald." said Naismith, "Both are unconcerned with strict realism when it comes to colour. They use colour to achieve drama and emotion with extremely vivid results." Naismith realised he had strayed from the original point of the conversation.

Dave saw his chance to broach the subject of Kessler's reputation. "Sam mentioned talk of Kessler's paintings having some kind of *aura*."

Naismith paused, "Aura? Well in a way that's another term for an uncertain form of energy. My limited understanding of auras, is of an essence that surrounds us? Some individuals believe they can see it, read its colours. I suppose it's not too much of an imaginative stretch when one thinks of all the invisible energy waves we all now know to exist- x rays, radio waves and such. With Kessler's paintings I suppose it's a case of cause and/or effect. A myth has grown around his work and who can say what substance lies at its heart? His work is captivating, I can vouch for that."

"Professor," Dave sat forward in his seat. "Since I started this investigation each image of Kessler's work I have viewed has had a...." he searched for the right words, "a deep effect on me, emotionally. Like a rush from a shot of a powerful drug. A moment of...... expanded consciousness... both exhilarating and frightening. It's like nothing I've experienced before, I can't explain it." Dave sat back and did not hide his sigh of relief at having voiced it.

Naismith leaned back into his tan leather chair removing his glasses and sucking on one of the ear curves. "Aura? Energy? Whatever one calls it," he said, "It sounds...as if through Kessler's paintings some unusually powerful telepathy is taking place. Somebody or something is communicating with you."

Raw Umber

As Dave Joseph drove home from his meeting with Professor Naismith his mind was scarcely on the road. In a sense it had been therapeutic to unburden what he had been experiencing - the sensations provoked by Kessler's artwork. In all other aspects, however, there were just a multitude of questions. Naismith's words kept reverberating in his head.

Somebody or something is communicating with you.

The concept itself unsettled Joseph. Could that be possible? It suddenly dawned on Joseph that up to now he had only viewed Kessler's art second generation – either online or through facsimile. If he was reacting so powerfully to the images in diluted form how would he respond to an original? Kate Sinclair's painting had none of its original content remaining so that would need to be discounted. What of that painting? Surely the lab must have come to some conclusions by now? Some hard physical evidence was what this case lacked, but Dave realised relying on the lab to provide this nugget was wishful thinking.

Most of the next day Dave found himself side tracked. With D.I. Leighton still out reports were stacking up. The investigations into cases with a Kessler connection would lack official support at this stage. Perhaps if Kate Sinclair had been attacked with a paintbrush yes, but not as things stood. Dave would have to continue his own enquiries as and when.

Snatching a sandwich at his desk Dave put in a call to Lieutenant De Caen at Direction Centrale de la Police Judiclare, Paris, who had worked on the Mantois killing. Despite a combination of Dave's schoolboy French and the lieutenant's thick accent the request for a jpeg image of the painting defaced with bloody text was agreed to. De Caen informed Dave the fashion designers lifestyle had made things difficult in identifying a suspect. The brutality of the attack led to theories of either a deeply embittered former lover or an unbalanced obsessive fan, clearly the perpetrator took pleasure in the man's suffering. The designer's home saw many comings and goings, being notorious for wild parties. Finger prints were numerous and other physical evidence was more consistent with that found at a brothel or a crack den, but isolating or eliminating any proved impossible. Apart from routine laboratory tests, specifically finger printing and DNA testing, the Kessler painting, Dave was told, had been catalogued and placed in evidence storage. The writing scrawled across it seemed to have drawn a blank, being largely indistinct. It had been assumed the perpetrator was venting their anger in the victim's blood. Dave thought how often jealous ex-lovers and the insane made for convenient scapegoats. De Caen was very cooperative though and with a closing Dave's French teacher at secondary school would have been proud of Joseph ended the call turning his attention to the computer.

The email and attached jpeg arrived in Dave's account. He immediately printed off an A4 copy. As the printer whirred into action he studied the image on screen. He felt no violent reaction this time, though he did find himself becoming lost in the patterns the writing formed. Like an aerial view of a maze he observed. He pondered if, like a maze, it too was a puzzle of sorts. Dave blinked; the Professor can handle this one he thought. He rolled the A4 printout into a tube, secured it with a rubber band, and tucked it into the inside pocket of his jacket, hanging on the coat stand.

Sitting again Dave picked up his phone looking at the business card he had exchanged yesterday with his own. *Professor Charles Naismith*, it read, *Lecturer in Art and Antiquity*. Being Wednesday Sam had her Reiki night get together with other fellow practitioners of the therapy, so Dave would enquire whether the Professor might meet up later for a drink.

With the working day drawing to a close the outer office

thinned of personnel; Dave closed his door to affect some privacy. Sitting in front of his PC he created a new document file, naming it *Kessler*. He began transferring all the information he had accrued: The Kate Sinclair report, information on the Mantois murder including the jpeg, press reports on the industrialist Levine's death, his burnt out factory and its surviving painting and articles on the Romanian orphanage and the *Salvation* effect. Completing this he noticed the PC's toolbar clock read 5:20pm; he moved the cursor to shutdown just as the office door was hurled open. A familiar voice mixed with the rattling glass.

"You miss me while I was gone?" D.I. Leighton, holding the door handle, face grinning, leaning in like a bulldog straining at its leash.

Aware he had exhibited shock Dave's hand withdrew from the mouse. "Court case over then?"

"Halle-bloody-lujah!" Leighton bellowed. "You'll be glad to know you have the pleasure of my company once more." Still hovering at the door the D.I. added, "I hear from His Bloody Highness you haven't totally steered the ship up shitcreek in my absence. Glad to see you at least haven't planted your arse at my desk with an eye on promotion. S'pose I should be glad of that!"

Dave knew that was the closest to a compliment he would receive for all his efforts. "Glad to have you back Guv, reports coming out of my ears. You want to see any now?"

"Not bloody likely!" Leighton snorted, "Anyway you're coming with me. We're off to the lab."

Stewart Fellows rarely looked more at home than in a lab. Pudding bowl hair and large simple gilt frame spectacles that were last available in any reputable optician when a mobile phone weighed the same as a house brick.

"It just makes no sense whatsoever," Fellows babbled, as he beckoned the D.I. and D.S. to follow him.

The two policemen exchanged glances as the little man marched them through to the main lab.

"It has to be seen to be believed," more babbling, "and as to what I write in my report?"

Even before reaching it Dave knew something about the painting had changed. He felt a now familiar, but stronger, warm pulsing glow bathe his rib cage. As Fellows pointed to the canvas Dave's flesh pimpled into cold mounds, the hairs feeling coarser as they prickled his skin. He could feel the blood coursing through every vessel in his body. Time seemed to slow, every sight and sound enhanced.

The painting looked as fresh as if it had been completed that day. The once damaged surface had completely healed, not a trace remained of its once thick sulphurous mask.

"Well!" said Leighton almost lost for words, "Butter me up and fuck me sideways".

With D.S. Joseph leaving the lab for home D.I. Leighton returned to the office. The altered appearance of the painting had dumbfounded the seasoned Inspector.

Joseph had admitted making some preliminary enquiries about the artist but Leighton's nose for the job and Joseph's alarm at his unexpected return had aroused the older man's suspicions. Joseph was withholding something; he knew it.

Leighton sat at Joseph's desk and jiggled the mouse, crackling the monitor to life, restoring it as Joseph had left it. With his neck craned forward Leighton explored the displayed files clicking open the one entitled *Kessler*. Loosening his tie he began reading the contents.

"There's actually something rather spooky about you going for a drink with my lecturer." Sam had joked, when Dave had told her who he was meeting.

Dave had discarded his shirt/tie combo, his usual C.I.D daywear, and changed into jeans and a navy blue t-shirt which accentuated his muscular frame, his short dark hair had been tamed with gel. His look still screamed *copper*.

"What if your lecturer was an attractive older woman and I was splashing Pacco Rabbane everywhere?" Dave had responded.

Sam agreed that would be an altogether worse prospect. As she was not drinking, Sam volunteered to drive Dave to the pub and pick him up later.

At 8:45pm she beeped the horn, waved, and left him at *The George*. The professor was already sat in a corner seat, a pint of Guinness in front of him. He saluted a greeting as Dave went to the bar, Dave gave a thumbs up and cupped his hand in the mime of asking if the professor wanted a drink, Naismith responded by holding his glass aloft. Ritual over Dave took his seat opposite the professor.

"Thanks for coming…I brought this for you…And also… I wanted to update you," Dave handed over the A4 roll of paper.

"I'm delighted you called. A welcome distraction." Naismith replied, "Glad to get away from my desk and the end of year paperwork. Ah now….what have we here?" Like an excited child at Christmas the professor loosened the scroll, rolled it across the table and used his pint to anchor one end. "The infamous Mantois painting, correct?"

Dave nodded, his pint glass at his lips.

"Most perplexing..." Naismith traced his finger over the images red text, imagining how it may have felt to create it in warm blood; he shivered. "This is hardly my field of expertise but I do have some colleagues at the museum- archaeologists, historians- who may be better informed?"

"The museum?" Dave raised an eyebrow.

"Another string to my bow! I do have a life away from Establishment!" Naismith smiled, "In fact…. I am currently involved in a very exciting dig in West Sussex, having a dreadful time with vandals though I'm afraid. Our security amounts to an overweight man, with an equally overweight dog, in a small van which visits, at best, twice nightly. Some of those involved in the project have taken to watching the site themselves for a few hours at a time, myself included."

Dave tried not to laugh," Catch anyone yet?"

"Alas not, but perhaps our presence has curtailed their night hawking."

Dave knew the phrase; rogue metal detectorists looking to plunder a site of its hidden treasure using the cover of darkness. "Anyone shows up, call the police, don't get all...... Indiana Jones on them!"

The Professor laughed and Dave laughed too; he couldn't quite imagine Naismith heroically cracking a whip. He looked much more the oak panelled library or quaint country pub type.

After a gulp of his Guinness and a repositioning of his spectacles Naismith returned to the printout which had rolled up on itself. As he made to smooth it flat the wall mounted light above revealed traces of the image through the paper's reverse side. "Hmm...." Naismith lifted the sheet to the light viewing it from behind.

Dave watched surprised and curious at the man's antics.

"Well, well.... I do believe..." Naismith's face was obscured by the paper. "...this text was written backwards."

Dave's attention focused, "What? Really? Can you decipher it?"

Naismith peered over the paper, "One step at a time Dear boy! It has the appearance of Latin... It's possible.... Certainly not classical Latin though...hmmm, Archaic perhaps...? Very curious indeed."

"Any way to confirm that? Work towards translating it?" Dave's voice was excited.

"I will ask around. May I show it to some associates?"

"Of course, I'd be grateful."

Looking at the paper right side up again, the Professor pursed his lips. "I think it may be a repeated phrase..... there is some considerable repetition in character use. In some areas it overlaps, in others it is more legible. It would be worth enhancing it digitally." Concern crossed the academics features,

"Something wrong Professor?

Naismith lowered the paper and removed his glasses. "You do know what one usually associates backward messaging with?"

Dave shrugged.

"Traditionally it is attributed to the diabolic, the *demonic*."

Dave didn't need to speak, his expression betrayed him.

"I know.... I know." the Professor admitted, "but I am an historian, you are a policeman. I can tell you categorically that throughout history there have been many recorded references relating to demonic activity and attacks".

"I'm sorry," Dave took a large sip of his lager. "If I tell my D.I. we're looking for a bright red guy with horns, goat's feet and an arrow for a tail, I'm on a one way ticket back to the beat; I've done my time as a plod."

"Indeed, but there may be a link….. perhaps a demonic cult? Satanists still exist. Who knows what crowd Mantois associated with? But to use Archaic Latin…..? Most unorthodox, one usually only hears of its use prior to 75 BC."

The two men sat listening to their own thoughts for a moment. Dave's mind reviewed the scant evidence relating to the cases. His chilled beer was poor comfort as he recalled the injuries to Sinclair, seemingly at the hands, or rather claws, of an unidentified attacker, the huge shattered pane of glass in her bathroom; her last act- the forming of the cross. And that painting…He had almost forgotten about its miraculous restoration in the lab. What too of his own recent experiences and sensations, as foreign as the archaic Latin Naismith spoke of. Dave sensed his drinking companion was probably considering the evidence he was aware of too, perhaps even formulating a theory which involved the supernatural.

Fighting all his police training, experience and rational thinking and taking a huge glug of alcohol Dave broke the silence, "If anyone asks I didn't say this, but tell me more about what you know concerning the *demonic*?"

Naismith lubricated his tonsils with alcohol and began, "Understood! First a point of accuracy, the word demon did not originally carry negative connotations. Prior to the spread of Christianity the word merely described any…..*supernatural* being. Pretty much every culture has its own folklore; demons often creeping into its art. This is where my knowledge comes from, unsurprisingly!" Naismith's eyes twinkled, "Hironymus Bosch, for example, painted… horrific visions of demons… contending for the souls of men. In his time evil was ever present."

Dave listened intently as a boy might to his father's bedtime storytelling.

"In Bosch's time..." Naismith continued, "Demons and damnation were *real*; understand it was a time of death and decay, anxiety and uncertainty, with people believing themselves..... on the brink of destruction. With the Antichrist expected these concerns dominated people's thoughts. The church reinforced this, continuously warning of the torment, humiliation and torture of Hell awaiting those who sinned. Little wonder demons appear so often in art and literature. With time however the Devil somewhat went out of fashion, becoming more allegorical. One finds oneself now in a less God fearing society, so for us it's easy to scoff at what our ancestors believed. We provide secular explanations for evil acts- insanity, addiction, nature/nurture, power, lust, envy. We still talk of *wrestling with our demons* but we are, in reality, talking of our own, internal, struggles. These days our obsessions are largely fixated on ourselves."

After a pause Naismith sighed. "I rather fear I have drifted from the point. Apologies, bad habit."

Dave smiled, "It's fine. I don't really know what I wanted to hear anyway... I've become so immersed in this investigation and yet I still seem to know so little."

"And these Kessler paintings?" Naismith remarked, "The power they seem to have over your emotional responses? Surely that has made your desire for answers one more than just professional?" Naismith could easily double for a psychiatrist.

Dave took a long deep breath and exhaled slowly. He was grateful for the professor's understanding and nodded.

"You are aware of the artist William Blake?" Naismith raised an eyebrow.

Dave shrugged, in the Professors company he felt more like a schoolboy by the minute.

"No matter." said Naismith "You can *Google* him I'm sure, should you so wish. Whilst painting, Blake attributed...bizarre sensory experiences to supernatural entities that, he claimed, visited him frequently. He was a deeply religious man, the Bible being his main inspiration, a great poet as well as a painter; he claimed some of his poetry had been dictated by angels! One of his greatest works - *The Good and Evil Angels* - sees two figures battling over a human child...one bathed in light from the sun rising behind him, the other engulfed by flames. The flames however shed no light... *Evil has cast his shadow across the earth...*" The professor paused for a drink and possibly for effect.

A trifle hammy Dave thought, but it worked. His bones were chilled.

"You recall my lecture on Divine Inspiration?"

Dave nodded, hoping he wouldn't be tested on it.

"Well, then you see the long and close relationship Art and the Divine share. Art has the capacity to communicate with us on a much deeper level than the obvious or the literal. I have spent my entire adult life studying art, attempting to extract the essence from each work, imagining myself in the mind of the artist, searching shared emotions, endeavouring to comprehend what drove him to cast his first brushstrokes on the canvas before him...." Naismith's voice had a musical lilt "....but I have yet to feel what you feel when you confront a Kessler.... It is a cause for wonder what *force* is responsible, why is Kessler's work so integral and more importantly I ask...is this *force* one of Good...or Evil?"

Dave felt the uncertainty and mysterious nature of the situation he found himself plunged into. Through Kessler's art was he really in some way being communicated with?

The professor broke Dave's train of thought. "Your news?"

"Huh?"

"You said you had an update?"

"Oh..." Dave stuttered, "I almost forgot, it's about the painting found at the Sinclair crime scene."

"Ah yes, has your lab discovered the manner in which it was destroyed?"

Dave downed the remainder of his pint, "Well, that's just it....um...it's not destroyed anymore".

As Naismith raised his eyebrows his spectacles slipped from his nose.

"Drink up Professor." Dave handed him his Guinness,

"You're going to need another of those."

Paynes Gray

From a brush loaded sticky wet with blue black, the moonlit forms of scarecrow limbed trees took shape. Alternate pressure of the artist's hand saw twisted broken branches seemingly reach from the canvas.

Professor Naismith had declined a lift home when Sam came to collect Dave. It was a walk home of no more than twenty minutes and would afford him time to stretch his legs.

The late June evening granted clear views of the city lights from the hill road. Due to the exposed nature of the location it was not unusual to feel a strong breeze but, as he continued on his journey, the Professor felt the need to pull his jacket around him and fasten it. This would also prevent the rolled up printout from escaping his inside pocket.

A landscape began to emerge as more tree forms filled the void; a dense, impassable, carbonised forest, the moon barely penetrating its heart. Tiny touches of Paynes Gray, flinty lunar highlights daring to shine in such a soulless place.

Dust dry topsoil from the hill had swept up and started to spiral around the Professor's feet as he picked up his pace. Now away from the main road, country lanes hooded by ancient oaks led his way. Street lamps stood sentry less frequently now offering up rare pools of welcome yellow. Naismith shivered. He tugged his collar up. Apart from the rustling of trees and hedgerows it was quite silent and yet he felt the need to turn, fearing on his path he was not alone.

"Paranoid..." he mused, still his unease intensified. The

temperature had dropped noticeably and the movement through the foliage around him had increased, the wind changing dramatically from one direction to another. Where there had once been sight of some stars and a sliver of moonlight there were merely heavy boughs looming low. And there was heaviness in the air, akin to the pressure only a violent storm could abate. But the Professor also felt the change in him not just around him. His head had started to throb; dizziness had thrown his feet clumsily off course. His blood felt as if it was altering in viscosity -coagulating in his veins- and the air tasted sour, contaminated. Naismith gasped, stumbling as he fought to keep moving forward, longing now for the sanctuary of home.

From foreground to horizon a tangle of charred, gnarled, silhouettes faded into an indigo sky. Kessler plunged the brush into a jar of turpentine, whisking it, squeezing the bristles against the side of the jar. Clouds of grey billowed, stealing the jar's contents of its purity.

What had started as a fresh breeze was now a vortex, compounding the Professor's disorientation and distress. His feet tripped, shoes scuffing, dumping him into thick bracken, tiny thorns hooking his clothes, tearing his face. Summoning precious strength, with a lurch, he freed himself from the myriad of barbs, hands bloodied and stinging raw. In the centre of his chest Naismith felt the tight grip he recognised as angina. He forced his body to stumble on, clutching at the site of his pain. Sucking at the stale air he felt the pressure spread to his throat and jaw, every remaining ounce of energy directed at moving toward the distant, guttering, streetlight, visible ahead. He dared not look behind him; he could feel his pursuer's presence- in an overwhelming sense of despair. While pain coursed the length of his left arm, details of a hundred paintings flashed in his mind, vibrant and vivid. A pained screeching seemed to shred at the tympanic membranes of his ears; the already tainted air now tasted thick and fermented. Above him the sky, dark and threatening, seemed enveloping, robbing him of hope. And yet, in the midst of contagious misery the Professor's mind settled on one modicum of comfort. From the vast catalogue of paintings stored in his brain one stood out as dominant, the image growing stronger and brighter.

The Liberation of St Peter by Raphael- two events shown in the one painting: an angel rousing the Saint and then leading him from prison. The theme: deliverance - a night scene illuminated by three separate sources: the moonlit sky, a burning torch and the saviour angel's supernatural aura.

Weak and in intense pain the Professor managed a smile. He patted at his jacket pockets searching...

The brush now clean, Kessler stood it, bristles upward, in a block of wood drilled with deep holes of varying thicknesses. He removed his round tortoiseshell framed glasses and rubbed the inside corners of his eyes. It was late and his eyes hurt. The painting would need to dry before he could add to it.

Naismith located the object of his hunt through his pockets; he pulled out the tiny silver pill box and with shaking hands removed one of the *Nitrostat*. He popped it under his tongue, instantly feeling it dissolve. Breathing hard he bent forward holding his knees, eyes closed, physically exhausted.

All was silent again. In an instant normality had returned and the Professor was in his street; a leafy lane full of homes to slumbering souls, blissfully unaware of the dark presence in their midst, blind even to the possibility of its existence.

Cadmium Yellow

A jog before work would help Dave make some sense of things, allow him some perspective, he kidded himself.

At 7:20am it was already hot, the sky cloudless. As his trainers pounded the tarmac path following the shoreline round Hilsea Creek and Tipner Lake he was already sweating through his grey t-shirt. His build was more muscular than athletic but he tried, of late, to focus on his cardiovascular health. As a copper he knew there were times when he may have to give chase and with Leighton as his D.I. that role would surely fall to Dave. Leighton broke a sweat tying his shoelaces! Right now being a copper didn't seem to offer much in the way of an advantage. So much police work was clear cut with established procedure but most of what had happened recently seemed abstract.

Portchester Castle was visible on the horizon across the expanse of swampy green water. Discarded tyres protruded from the slime like giant croquet hoops. Until recently there had been a decommissioned submarine in the same waters, adding to the already surreal landscape. In its own way this place was weirdly beautiful- hardly a compliment Dave thought, if applied to a person, but appropriate here. He was surprising himself, he often jogged this route, but rarely had he noticed it in such detail. Maybe the Professor's enthusiasm had rubbed off on him? Naismith had certainly given Dave plenty cause for thought. After discussing the miraculous restoration of the Kate Sinclair painting he and Professor had talked Kessler. Though the artist had links with the university, having written a large cheque for the art wing build, Naismith had only met him once before. The Kessler wing had only been completed two years ago and last year had been the first year the artist had attended the end of year exhibition, awarding his gold prize to the student's work he most admired. No preliminaries. He arrived, viewed, awarded and left. This was all to happen again next week. Sam had been getting more excited by the day with high hopes for her *RockPool* study. When Dave had asked what he knew of Kessler, Naismith had answered, *Who can know Kessler? He himself says he can only be truly known through his paintings.* Naismith had added that Kessler rarely made public appearances, perhaps important exhibitions, or first nights of ballets / theatre productions he had designed sets or costumes for, but these were exceptions. An enigma! Just what I need, Dave thought.

Around him other people were appearing, starting their day; Dave continued on towards the derelict Lido. Dogs were being let from their leads, yapping excitedly, serious cyclists clad head to toe in lycra whizzed by on the split path, two lanes to avoid collisions.

Joseph had known this area since childhood. As a kid he had visited regularly with his parents. There must be photos somewhere… in dusty leather covered albums- Happy times, all too brief, he with a brightly coloured net on a bamboo stick skimming the water for crabs. Summers of bike rides, 99 ice creams, flying kites. Memories that now seemed so distant they hardly seemed to be his.

Dave turned for home.

Manganese Blue

Professor Naismith hissed through his teeth and winced. He dabbed the surgical spirit soaked cotton wool ball over the criss cross scratches on his face. As he stared in the mirror he still felt the residue of last nights fear, his hands still trembled. He grasped the edges of the sink and took a deep breath. Where previously *Divine inspiration* had dominated his thoughts, *Divine intervention* had taken its place.

Detective Chief Superintendent Ian Steele placed the phone receiver back in its cradle. His thick, prematurely grey hair made him resemble the *before* picture of a hair dye ad. On the desk in front of him was a copy of the morning edition of *The Herald*, the subject of which had caused the right royal bollocking he had just received from his superior, and now it was his turn to pass it down the line.

Leighton and Joseph joined the others in the outer office. The murmurs of disquiet were broken as D.C.S. Steele took his place in front of the whiteboard.

"If I may have your attention..." the volume and firmness in his tone demanded respect. "I *will* keep this brief...."

"There *is* a God," Leighton mumbled, ventriloquist like, in an aside to Dave.

Steele's eyes narrowed as he continued, "In today's *Herald*," he said, holding his copy aloft, "I find an article by our local crime reporter, Sarah Nash, informing the world that the death of Kate Sinclair has.... and I quote.... *links to the mysterious Kessler curse.*" Steele's pale blue eyes scanned the watching faces. "The article goes on to rehash archive material on the said *Kessler Curse Mysteries* and reminds locals that *the reclusive artist will be making a rare appearance at our university next week.*"

Joseph's stomach lurched. How the hell had Nash got that story? An article like this could potentially make a mockery of any serious investigation. Throw the words *mystery* and *curse* at the public and you may as well assign Scooby Doo to the case!

"I need not remind you all of the consequences in breaching confidentiality and leaking information to the press. I will have no hesitation in taking immediate action, using the full office of my authority, and suspending anyone found responsible for this or any other unauthorised information reaching the media." Steele turned toward Joseph and Leighton. He curled his index finger to beckon them, "If I might have a private word?" He gestured to the newspaper, "You might want to bring that with you?"

D.C.S. Steele took his position of authority in the black leather chair behind his desk. He motioned the D.I. and D.S. to sit. "As you are heading up the Sinclair investigation D.I. Leighton, I'm sure you are aware of your responsibility in how the case should proceed. Shortly I will have to dignify this..." he pointed to the newspaper.... "this *tripe* with an official response."

"Sir, you'll appreciate up until yesterday I've been sat on my arse tied up in court." Leighton said, immediately distancing himself, I'm sure though that D.S. Joseph will be able to bring you up to speed with any progress."

"I say again, D.I. Leighton, it is *your* responsibility, and from now on *you* will *get up to speed* and regularly keep me briefed as to developments." Steele's voice was uncompromising. He turned to D.S. Joseph, "What, if any of this hyperbole has any basis in truth?"

Dave had read Nash's article on route to Steele's office. He cleared his throat. "Well sir, as you know due to the unusual and unexplained damage to the Kessler painting at the scene I did some preliminaries on Kessler himself and, in the course of that, I explored previous incidents linked to his paintings. There are no clear cut conclusions in any of the cases; I believe there are some striking elements, but nothing that points directly to a suspect or a motive." Dave opted for damage control, hoping a calm, reasoned approach was what the Chief Super was seeking.

"So this hatchet job is just sensationalist hokum?" Steele relaxed a little.

"Sir...." Dave began," In what I have discovered there are a lot of questions that remain unanswered. You've been made aware of the paintings dramatic restoration?"

"Yes indeed," Steele searched a pile of printouts. "The lab sent me more details this morning. Fellows says the original damage was... *likely caused by an extreme surge of unknown energy...*"

"What the bloody hell is that?" Leighton spluttered.

Steele continued. "......*Residue, on analysis contained high levels of sulphur.* Fellows draws our attention to similar residue found at the scene on the broken window and the victim's wounds." Steele skimmed the printout..... "*Painting now shows no physical or chemical trace of residue and can offer no explanation of its appearance and / or subsequent disappearance.*"

Dave leaned forward in his chair, "So you see Sir? This is a far from usual investigation."

"Go on" Steele said.

"In order to make any progress I suggest following up on *any* lead - even if it means suspending our disbelief. Kessler is of interest, remarkable things have happened to his paintings and to some of the people around them." Dave was of course privately including himself in that company. He could see Leighton's head shaking in disapproval and so could Steele,

"Have you something to say D.I. Leighton?"

"I don't want to be party to a bloody wild goose chase that risk making me the laughing stock of the division. The painting's not significant. Sinclair probably pissed someone off...ripped 'em off too, I don't doubt. They cut her up and then confused the crime scene, breaking the window and....I don't know, pissed on her precious painting. Probably perfectly reasonable explanations for the other *Kessler curse* stories too. This sensationalism sells papers, no one actually believes it! Deny it Sir and distance yourself, that's how to come out smelling of roses. Stick to the facts."

Steele looked from one man to the other. In their own way each had something to offer, how they would pull together was another matter.

"Gentlemen, I will advise the press we are exploring every avenue and instruct them not to hamper the investigation any further with wild speculation. D.S. Joseph you're right - this is a very unusual case and therefore requires some thinking *outside the box* and you have my support in doing so. D.I. Leighton I hope you can indeed find a reasonable explanation to bring this case to a close. I somehow think that will be difficult having reviewed the sparse evidence, but I know you never shy away from a challenge. Thank you gentlemen."

Dave was pleased at least to have some official support, Leighton however clenched his fists as he rose to leave, in his eyes he had been undermined.

Indigo

"AH..ah!" Dave rebuked, kissing Sam on the cheek, "Stop fiddling!"

Reluctantly Sam lowered the paint brush and frowned at the canvas.

"Do I have to confiscate that?" Dave made to grab at the brush.

Sam whisked it away with a smile.

Dave cupped his hands to his mouth affecting a megaphone, "You there... yes you... the devastatingly attractive female in the throwback to the 1970's blouse......PUT THE BRUSH DOWN AND STEP AWAY FROM THE CANVAS." He lowered his hands, "I'm going in Sarge, cover me....." in feigned slow motion Dave made an overly dramatic stretch, grasping and twisting the brush from Sam's hand as if disarming her.

"Okay... okay!" Sam held her hands up, "I get the hint!"

Dave dabbed her nose with the bristles leaving it Smurf blue, "Oops..Sorry!"

"DAAAAVE!" Sam complained as she started to laugh.

"I'm doing you a favour love; a good artist knows when to stop, isn't that what you always say? It looks terrific. Let it dry and get it to Uni, the clocks a-ticking woman!"

Sam smiled, "I know... you're right, it's just....it's a great opportunity, catch Kessler's eye, get some positive feedback."

"Hmm." Dave cleaned the brush twirling the bristles in an old marmalade jar filled with turps. "Not sure catching Kessler's eye is an entirely good thing."

Sam laughed, "You're just as excited to meet him as I am – admit it!"

"Curious," Dave answered, hiding the fact there were actually butterflies in his stomach as he thought of confronting the artist.

"Ex-cited." Sam corrected, "I know you have your reservations but keep an open mind yeh?"

Dave tweaked the bristles into a fine point, "There! Just how you like it."

"Perfect! You know if you ever tire of policing you're welcome to be my brush twizzler! By the way, how much did you and the Professor drink last night?"

Dave opened the fridge and peered in, "Few pints. Why?"

"He looked rough as a badgers arse, face all scratched up, couple of plasters on his chin."

"Strange," Dave took a bottle of rose' from the shelf, "He was fine when we left him....you want some plonk; we still have some of those bottles we got on offer?"

"Sure... Why not give him a call? He looked shocking when I saw him!"

Dave grabbed his mobile and found Naismith's number having entered it into memory. "Professor? It's Dave Joseph, you ok?"

Sarah Nash sat at her favourite window position in *The Coffee Bean*, her laptop open in front of her, a large latte by its side. She toyed with the ornate dangly earring in her right ear as she watched life go on about her through the window. *Poor saps*, she thought as shoppers struggled with groceries. Nash rarely shopped and never cooked, mainly eating out and usually claiming on expenses. The editor didn't complain- articles like the *Kessler Curse* racked up sales. She had a diverse range of *sources* and expenses wining and dining them proved solid investment.

Her mobile rang, vibrating its way across the table. She snapped it up.

"Sarah Nash."

A familiar voice on the other end made her smile.

"Did you like it?" She goaded.

Nash held the phone away from her ear as the caller vented.

"Thank you so much for the exclusive Honey – I'm ever so grateful, very public spirited." There was a little girl lost in her playful tone, guaranteed to grate.

More ranting vented through the mobile.

"Now you will let me know any further developments wont you? Nash's voice instantly became cold, "It would be such a shame to jeopardise our close working relationship. Who knows what I'd be driven to do. I might feel a need to reveal all sorts of things in a bid to relieve my conscience. Knowing so much and being able to say so little, such a heavy burden!" She blinked at the response but she had been called much worse, often in fact.

The caller, empty of threats, hung up.

Nash placed her phone beside her laptop and, taking advantage of the WiFi available, accessed the internet. Her perfect acrylic nails glinted with reflected sunlight as she *Google* searched -

Images- *Kessler*

Terre Verte

Dave was back in the lecturer's office. Naismith's face looked like someone had been playing noughts and crosses on it.

"Whoa.... you look like you've been through the wars Professor."

"Everyone loses sympathy when I tell them I sustained my injuries walking home from the pub," Naismith smiled a half smile.

"PFO." Dave stated.

"I'm sorry?"

"Pissed, fell over," Dave answered, "police shorthand!"

"Ah, I fear that's what it seems but as I intonated in our phone call there was rather more to it than that."

Dave sat down. "Now you've had a couple of days to think it over, how can you best describe what happened, you said you felt…. *pursued*?"

"Yes, Oh, this is going to sound very overdramatic……pursued yes, by a… wretched… evil presence…. determined to steal all goodness or hope a man holds in his heart. We spoke before about energy….. This was an energy capable of harnessing the elements- making conspirators of them in its terror. A dark.. malevolent force, the like of which I do not wish to ever face again.." the professor took a ragged breath, " I fear I sound mad?"

Dave could see the genuine suffering Naismith had endured and having experienced powerful reactions to unexplained forces himself of late, he could empathise. "You didn't see anything?"

Naismith shuddered, "Thank God no, I hesitate to imagine what form such wanton evil could take. To feel it was enough."

"Are you sure you're...ok?"

"Thanks to Raphael and Saint Peter, yes."

Dave tilted his head inviting elaboration.

"In what I thought might be my last breaths on this earth it wasn't my life that flashed before me, but rather many of the paintings I have seen. It made me acutely grateful that I am capable of appreciating such beauty, am able to inspire others to feel the same, and to make a living from my passion." Naismith's eyes regained some former sparkle, "As I fought for breath a picture appeared to me with such....clarity, such divine beauty, the inherent goodness in it instilling hope once more to my soul."

To anyone else, D.I. Leighton especially, this would have had them reaching for the straight jacket, but to Dave it all made perfect sense. *Art had power*.

"To business!" Naismith wheeled his chair toward the computer desk whilst still seated in it, his feet propelling his journey in claw toed steps. Dave watched as he fiddled with his glasses and navigated the cursor across the screen. "I took the liberty of contacting a restorer at the National Gallery through one of my museum cohorts. I know they have the technology to dramatically enhance images. They use it to discover a paintings original colour and detail and reveal what lies beneath centuries of dirt and discoloured varnish - It's not unusual to find a blonde where one assumed there was a brunette!" The professor brought up the image of the Mantois painting on the screen. He hit print and the image started to appear on an A4 sheet emerging from the printer nearby. Dave retrieved it from the tray and studied it.

"The original image has been altered to compensate for the fact the text was originally written backwards? All terribly clever stuff! You see how essentially it forms a repeated phrase?" Naismith printed another sheet, this time the copy of an email. "And this," he continued, "Courtesy of Professor Owen Eldridge at the British Museum, is our translation from the Archaic Latin!"

Dave watched as the email started to appear in print....the British Museum header...the opening gambit and pleasantries, and then indented in speech marks and typed in capitals,

"THEIR END WILL BE WHAT THEIR ACTIONS DESERVE."

Dave looked at the black text, a chill catching him unawares. "Wow, Professor, you've really excelled yourself, thank you. What do you make of this?"

"For what its worth – it's a biblical quote – *Corinthians 11:15* to be precise!"

"Really?" Dave watched as Naismith scooted himself back to behind his desk.

"Written backwards, as it was, I'd say it was *mocking* the bible, misusing the message twisting its sense." The professor touched lightly at one of his face scratches.

"I wonder what *actions* could *deserve* Mantois's fate." Dave asked, taking his seat again.

"And one wonders what manner of vigilante dispensed such a singular form of justice?" Naismith added.

Dave looked as the Professor lightly dabbed one of many angry cuts. "Perhaps you know better than anyone the answer to that one."

Dave hadn't expected D.I .Leighton to be impressed with the deciphering of the Mantois painting. The response?

"Ask me it confirms it was some nutter - a bloody bible bashing nutter. The worst kind of nutter! It's not our bloody case anyway. What did I say about a bloody wild goose chase?"

When it came to Leighton, Dave was thick skinned. The D.I. was an old school copper, brutish, unsubtle and with a gallows sense of humour, but his bludgeoning approach could prove damned effective at times. Subtlety, tact and diplomacy had their place but sometimes you needed a bull like Leighton to simply charge at a situation.

Surprisingly enough Leighton had, for him, been fairly civil since the meeting with the Chief Super. He was quite content to busy himself with other case reports while Dave collated as much as he could on the Sinclair case.

The Corinthians quote message could easily apply to

Kate Sinclair too. Miss Sinclair's *actions* had been proved to be underhand at best, often illegal.

When coroner's reports from her and Mantois were compared the claw like wounds proved eerily similar. Dave had no doubt now there was a link

Unbeknown to D.I. Leighton Dave had asked for, and been granted, a brief meeting with D.C.S. Steele.

"How may I help D.S. Joseph?" Steele sipped tea from his *Worlds best Dad* mug, a Fathers Day gift from his one year old boy.

"You're aware of my interest in Tybalt Kessler? In connection to the Sinclair killing?"

"Yes, and so is Miss Nash at *The Herald* regrettably. Tread very carefully down that path." Steele answered.

"Well, chance has it I have an invite to the University art exhibition he is judging in a few days time. My girl friend is exhibiting."

"I see ... and what is it you want from me?"

"Your permission to ask for an interview?" Dave knew he had no grounds to seek the artist's cooperation.

"I have no objection in you asking, it wholly depends on Kessler's willingness though. Certainly the strange transformation of his painting warrants investigation in relation to the Sinclair killing. Perhaps that should form the basis of your questioning. He is sure to be aware of Nash's article and its ... suggestions and insinuations, so be discreet. I know this is something within your capabilities ... unlike some fellow detectives!" Steele hid his smile as he drained his mug of its brew.

"Understood Sir. Thank you." Dave handed Steele the printouts outlining the Mantois case, the text translation and requested pathology report. "Thought you'd like to be made aware of this too Sir. D.I. Leighton doesn't support my line of enquiry, but I think in the light of the press interest, you should be possessed of the details."

Steele perused the information pausing on the biblical

quote. "More religious imagery ..." he continued reading, "And the same savagery ...What on earth is capable of inflicting such carnage?"

And then suddenly Dave found himself seven years old again ... standing at the doorway to the lounge of his family home. His grandmother smelling of scented talc holding him close. On the cornflower blue carpet laid his parents, blood pooling ruby red, and the thick scent of death penetrating his nostrils. The glint of a long kitchen knife's steel blade between them, the tiny silver cross just visible in his mother's outstretched hand. The tight protective hug from his grandmother's arms – the sound of her anguished sobs ...

"D.S. Joseph?" Steele's voice.

Dave zoned back in "Sir?"

"Is that all I can help you with?"

"Yes Sir, Thank you ..." Dave gathered his thoughts.

Steele added, "Let me know how you get on at the exhibition – and good luck to your girlfriend."

Dave felt like someone was whispering to him from a long, dark tunnel. A weak signal was trying to be heard.

Gold Ochre

The day of the University end of year art showcase exhibition arrived. Students had spent the morning hanging their work in the Kessler funded *Art Space* studio. Kessler had been generous enough to supply some cases of wine from his vineyard. A table had been set up with wine glasses with a small chiller nearby. With all the preparations complete students were released at 2:00pm and asked to be back for 6:00pm, suitably dressed and ready. Many took the opportunity for an extended late liquid lunch. There was an excited buzz, the anticipation of Kessler's appearance adding hugely to the already frayed nerves coming from displaying work to friends, family, perhaps even potential agents and buyers. Sam knew getting sloshed in the afternoon was not a wise idea. She bubbled with nervous energy as she sat in the pub with fellow students, sipping at her tall lime and soda. The exhibition pretty much brought to a close her and her fellow students' time at the University. She had got on well with everyone; it was usually in Sam's nature to do so. Some students lacked her discipline, coasting their way through the course, often begrudging deadlines for assignments – but not Sam. She happily lived and breathed Art, through it she expressed herself best, exploring and developing her talent in the process. For some students this may have been the end of their artistic life, harsh realities might well side track them into other careers but Sam was determined, for her, this was just the beginning.

Sam looked at her watch, "Guys ..." she said taking her last sip of lime flavoured fizzy soda, "I'm going to blast. I want to go home and change."

The company shouted their departing words raising their glasses, all full of alcohol induced high spirits.

Sam would miss this crowd.

Not unusually Dave was running late. He had rushed home, washed, changed into the suit Sam had laid out on the bed along with a suitable shirt and tie, thrown on some black shoes he suspected Sam had polished, and made for the University.

Arriving at the main entrance a sandwich board and a series of arrows led him to the *ArtSpace* studio. As he walked briskly towards the door he became aware of two people loitering. One obviously a press photographer, his Nikon armed with flash unit, and the unmistakable figure of Sarah Nash from the *Herald*.

Fuck, he thought, *What the hell are they doing here?* Of course he knew the answer – to ambush Kessler and drag up the whole *Curse* story and have it play out again in tomorrow's edition. Dave's first impulse was to warn her off but she had every right to be there, she would only claim she was covering the event anyway. Luckily for Dave, although he recognised her, she was unaware of his identity so, with that knowledge, he threw a smile and entered the studio.

Sam threw a frantic wave and Dave approached her, his hands raised in apology. "Sorry, sorry ... work." He kissed her.

"I'm just glad you're here. I'm so ner-vous!" Sam hugged him. Behind her, hanging on the wall, was her painting *RockPool* with its neatly typed card beside it.

"It looks amazing Sam ..." Dave's face was beaming admiration, "Don't you think?"

Sam toyed with a spiral curl of her hair, head tilted, as she looked at her work. If she had had a brush she would still be tinkering.

Dave laughed, "It looks AMAZING." he repeated, and then he whispered "You'll blow the competition out of the water."

"It's an *exhibition* not a competition!" Sam emphasized.

"Then why you so nervous?" Dave teased, giving her another hug.

"Detective Joseph," the familiar tones of Professor Naismith broke Dave's hold.

"Evening Professor. You all ready for your *royal visit*?"

Dave kept an arm around Sam's waist as he greeted Naismith.

The Professors scratches had noticeably healed allowing him a proper shave. He sported a cream linen suit, blue shirt and striped tie and neat brown brogues. He pulled up a sleeve and, needing to pull his glasses on from their chain, peered at his watch. "Our esteemed guest is due very shortly! I had better go wait outside in readiness I think."

Dave gestured to the door. "You do know you've got a reporter and photographer lying in wait for him? I'm afraid that's Sarah Nash – she's bound to try and cause trouble."

"Oh heavens." the Professor frowned. "That's not what we need at all. Kessler's doing us a huge favour attending."

"Do you want me to wait with you?" Dave asked, then turning to Sam, "If that's ok with you Sam?"

Sam smiled. "Of course, but you are off duty you know!"

Naismith replied. "If you wouldn't mind, yes, thank you that would be most appreciated given the circumstances."

Dave kissed Sam's forehead. "Come on then Prof. let's go line the red carpet".

As the two men made for the door Dave called back. "I'll check out the competition on my return!"

Sam blushed as Dave playfully poked out his tongue.

Dave watched as the photographer test fired his flash unit. Sarah Nash, meanwhile, applied a retouch of lip gloss, moving her lips together in a grimace to ensure an even coating.

Ensuring he was out of earshot Dave turned to Naismith. "How have you been Professor?"

"I admit thus far I haven't ventured out after dark." Naismith looked up at the sky, still June blue.

"No walking home tonight then!" Dave smiled.

"And how are *you* feeling … at meeting the man whose paintings seem to be communicating with you?" Naismith asked with an eyebrow raised.

Dave exhaled through bellowed cheeks, "I don't

know……. excited……curious…..nervous?"

"Scared even?" The Professor prompted.

"Hmm …" Dave answered, "I'll let you know!"

With that a sleek, black, Jaguar smoothly drew up, parking in the reserved space in front of the studio building. The tinted windows showed only silhouettes of a driver and a back seat passenger. The photographer moved in, camera pressed to his face, and Nash pulled at her handbag removing a Dictaphone. As Naismith stepped forward Dave formed a human shield his arms outstretched, palms out.

"They've hired a bloody bouncer." Nash hissed.

Dave twisted his head, now desperately eager to see the vehicle's passenger; his heart pumped hard, his breathing rate accelerated. It was like the bitter sweet anticipation of a first date, multiplied by a million.

The photographer pushed forward leaning his weight into Dave. His flash unit fired, the bright light momentarily bleaching Dave's vision. Dave held his ground. The car's driver had exited from the vehicle and now opened the rear passenger door.

Tybalt Kessler emerged.

Dave half glanced at the artist, one eye defensively still on Nash and the photographer. A long lost feeling from youth forgotten overcame him; he felt shy… awkward….wanting to look but not wanting to reveal his overwhelming emotion with inappropriate over interest. He was quite simply star struck. And to a huge degree.

Kessler's appearance did not disappoint. Dressed in an immaculately cut black two piece suit, red silk visibly lining the jacket, against a black shirt lay a slim multicoloured mosaic pattern tie. He stood just over 6ft. tall. His hair was a dark buzz cut, his skin a mocha tan; touches of grey flecked a short stubble beard. His eyes were alert, intelligent- bright swimming pool blue; a smile wrinkled his face, deep furrows across his brow. There was an inexplicable personal magnetism that radiated from him. Dave could feel the energy.

"Professor Naismith, how welcome it is to see you," the voice was deep, mellifluous, the trace of an accent. Swedish, Dave assumed.

"Thank you so much for attending." Naismith responded as the two men shook hands.

Dave blinked hard. *Look but don't look.* His body stiffened as the photographer attempted to push towards Kessler, the flash firing once more.

"Have you any comment on the recent local murder, one of a series of events linked to your paintings Mr. Kessler?" Nash's shrill voice rang across the car park.

Dave threw her disapproving look, still keeping himself between her and the artist.

Naismith offered an apology as he escorted Kessler towards the door.

"No comment to make on the so-called *Kessler Curse* then?" Nash further provoked.

As they reached the door Kessler calmly turned to her.

"I don't believe we have had the pleasure? Miss ….?"

"Sarah Nash, *The Herald*," came the proud answer.

"Ah..yes, Miss Nash," Kessler smiled, " I owe you my gratitude." He bowed slightly. "Thanks largely to your previous article, and its subsequent syndication, my agent informs me my name is close to topping internet searches nationally, and even making some impression globally. You are making an *enigma* of me. I had best increase my productivity to capitalise on this success, no?"

Clearly rattled Nash thrust her Dictaphone closer. "What of the killings associated with your paintings?"

"Well..." Kessler considered. "Paintings are like children. My role is one of conceiving and shaping them. Once they are fully formed and move into the wide world they become the concerns of others. Once they leave my sphere of influence surely how can I be held responsible?"

Nash stuttered and stammered, unable to structure a suitable response.

"Now if you will excuse me? I am looking forward to

discovering the talents of those awaiting me within - I assume with your preferring to be *outside* your readership has little or no interest in such aesthetics? Therefore may I be bold as to suggest you have little to gain in remaining?" With that Kessler moved through the door Naismith held open. Dave followed behind.

Kessler had exceeded expectation.

Where there had been excited jabbering and a general hubbub, hush descended on the studio. All eyes were directed toward Kessler. The artist seemed unfazed, smiling warmly in response, the Professor ushering him towards university hierarchy. Dave smiled as he saw the dejected expression of Sarah Nash through the plate glass door. Kessler's duelling had been admirable. The nervous anticipation, tinged with trepidation, Dave had felt in meeting the artist had transformed rapidly to respect for the man. Sam waved, beckoning Dave to join her again. Kessler meanwhile was being introduced to a line of fixed grins, Naismith in his role as Master of Ceremonies.

"So…. what do you think?" Sam asked, "I think he's rather dishy!"

"Hmm…he's a charmer that's for sure." Dave answered, "And he made mincemeat of Sarah Nash out there, for that alone I've got to like him."

"Not what you expected?" Sam quizzed. "Look at that smile…and those eyes… they could melt steel!"

"All right Dear. Keep your knickers on!" Dave laughed, "I don't know what I expected to be honest. Artists are such a weird bunch!"

"Ha ha." Sam answered as Dave leant in and kissed her.

"C'mon then Missy - show me around, educate my artistically challenged mind?" Dave grabbed her by the waist, "Actually sod that - how about a glass of vino?"

Once Kessler had greeted the University dignitaries, Naismith accompanied him in touring the works on show. Students had been instructed not to *hover,* whilst Kessler viewed, so it was common place to see them anxiously looking on from a safe distance, like spectators at a fireworks display. Kessler gave little away; he examined each artwork with interest sharing his observations with Naismith. The Professor would listen, then scribble in his tiny notebook and the two men would proceed on to the next picture.

Sam resisted the overwhelming urge to bite her fingernails to the quick as Kessler approached *RockPool*. Instead she sipped nervously at her glass of rosé.

"Stop being a worrywart! He's gonna love it," Dave reassured her.

"Oh God - he's seen it - he's seen it." Sam held her hand over her mouth to stop herself burbling further. Dave held her close.

Kessler took a step back, viewing the painting in its entirety. Inaudible, he spoke to Naismith who nodded sagely and jotted an entry in his book. Kessler then made a large sweeping movement with his hands in front of the canvas; Naismith nodded several times in approval then the two men moved on.

"What was that all about?" Dave asked.

Sam removed her hand from her mouth. "Search me. He seemed to like it though right?"

"Of course he did Doughnut! Tell you what if he doesn't … I'll arrest him - how's that?"

"On what charge?" Sam asked.

"Poor taste!"

Professor Naismith completed his speech, thanking exhibitors and those attending as well as key University staff, and finally turned to Kessler.

"We owe so much to our distinguished guest. He has provided everything from the very foundations upwards in the facility in which we stand today. Through his generosity and support we are able to nurture new artistic talent, provide state of the art resources, and thus ensure a new generation of artists thrive. We thank him and so does the future of Art.

And now to the Tybalt Kessler Gold Prize for Outstanding New Talent. I should now like to hand over to our esteemed guest and patron to announce this year's recipient. Ladies and Gentlemen, Mr Tybalt Kessler."

The assembled crowd joined in applause as Kessler took centre stage.

"Thank you Professor Naismith for your kind words and for your diligence in enabling students to create such inspiring works as we have enjoyed this evening. The award I am to present singles out a particular work from many I have enjoyed. It was a choice made largely on instinct as are most choices I make in life; a work of *powerful, positive, energy*."

Dave felt the words reflect his own experience of late.

Kessler continued. "The winner of this year's award goes to............ Sam Paris for *RockPool*."

Sam half shrieked, clasping her mouth with both hands, eyes wide.

Dave grinned as he prized her hands from her face. "You did it ... Didn't I tell you?" he kissed her.

Naismith was beckoning her to come forward.

"Oh - My - God!" Sam straightened her clothing, took a calming breath and approached Kessler.

"Congratulations." Kessler handed Sam the award - a gold-medallion nesting in a red silk lined velvet box. "Your work radiates an exquisite purity. One can almost feel the smoothness of the stones, sense the healing coolness of the water. Achieving such an evocative response sings of great talent."

"Thank-you...Thank-you so much," Sam replied, tears welling up.

"Here." Professor Naismith offered the blue silk handkerchief from his jacket pocket. "Well done Sam, I'm so pleased for you."

Sam dabbed her eye as she smiled at the two men.

Dave had moved forward, holding his mobile up in front of him. "How bout a picture?"

Kessler agreeably posed, smiling as he handed the prize to Sam. Applause filled the hall as Dave proudly took his picture.

"Perhaps one by the painting? Naismith suggested.

As Sam viewed the photos on Dave's phone, pleasantly surprised she didn't look like a simpering mess, Dave went to fetch celebratory drinks. The bartender for the night was barely coping with demand for free wine on offer.

"You want a hand mate?" Dave offered, as the bartender tried to uncork a fresh bottle.

"Cheers - appreciate that." The bartender, a hospitality student, tossed Dave a corkscrew, "If you could open one of each?"

Dave smiled, he had jumped from bouncer to bar keep in one evening, maybe it was time for a career change? Without looking at the bottles he popped the corks free, then, remembering he had actually come over to collect drinks, he noted the labels. He lifted the rose' bottle. The labels all featured the graphic of a chateau, complete with round tower, presumably Kessler's. In the foreground vines weaved in differing colours – green denoting white wine, red for the reds, pink on the rose bottle Dave held. Studying the label: the imposing chateau, the sinuous vines, he was reminded of fairytales - a beautiful landscape belying a sinister threat. He recognised from his rapidly growing physical response to the label the artist himself had designed it. A sudden surge of adrenalin loosened his grip on the bottle and he felt it slip from his sweaty palm. Before he could counteract the chilled bottle left his grasp. Closing his eyes awaiting the inevitable crash Dave heard instead the rich, deep timbre of Kessler's voice.

"A particularly fine vintage ...." Somehow, in some way, the artist had caught the falling bottle, "... too good to waste, no?"

Dave made a poor act of composing himself, rubbing his sweaty palms on his jacket. "Sorry, slipped straight out of my hands ..."

"Quite alright, plenty more......." Kessler extended his hand.

Dave shook it, glad his palms were dryer. "Dave Joseph" he said in introduction.

Kessler poured the wine into glasses on the table as he spoke, "You know your girlfriend has extraordinary vision."

Unsure as to how to answer, Dave opted for, "Thanks."

Sam was now talking to some university friends unaware of the meeting taking place. Dave's nervous state was calming somewhat, Kessler's calming voice strangely soothing. "It means the world to her ...." Dave continued, "Winning the award. She'll be walking on air for days - weeks." Dave smiled as he watched Sam excitedly chatting, showing the medal to her friends.

"A most deserved winner, no doubt," Kessler added.

Dave noticed the depth of colour in the artist's eyes, as vibrant a hue as he had seen all night in the artworks surrounding him. Dave felt more self assured. "Ha - I kept getting told it was an *exhibition* not a *competition*!"

Kessler laughed "Nonsense .... But most endearing."

"Yeah .... Dave agreed, looking over at Sam, fondness in his eyes.

"I wanted to thank you, for your assistance outside, on my arrival." Kessler said.

Dave faced him, "You're welcome, and anyway you handled yourself fine with no need of assistance."

Kessler laughed again, "I confess to enjoying putting Miss Nash back in her box. I wonder how she will contort my words to her advantage tomorrow in *The Herald*?"

"Hmm." Dave sipped some rose,' "I'm sure her poison pen will find some angle."

Kessler was helping himself to some of his own red, "I confess also to quizzing Professor Naismith on you somewhat?"

"Ah," Dave replied, "and what did you learn?" A little anxiety returned.

Page 59

"That you are a police detective investigating one of the crimes Miss Nash talked of, that you have researched the other *incidences*, that you have an *interest* in me ... and my work?" Kessler relayed it all with a matter of fact manner showing no hint of displeasure.

"Guilty as charged!" Dave joked, he decided to take a risk, "And did Professor Naismith also mention I would welcome your help?"

Kessler lowered his glass, "He ... *hinted* as much. The Professor would not wish to offend me I think."

"Would you agree in talking to me?" Dave pursued, "You are under no obligation of course, but there are many things I would like to discuss with you, it could be of great help I think."

Kessler thought, then spoke, "I am here in Portsmouth for a few more weeks, the chateau is undergoing some renovations - the perils of owning a fifteenth century property! You could visit my studio? So long as you don't mind my continuing to work as we converse?"

"Not at all, whatever works for you." Dave's heart raced in anticipation.

"Would the day after tomorrow be convenient?" Kessler took a wallet from his jacket.

"That would be great. Thank you."

Kessler pulled a business card from his black leather wallet and handed it over. It listed his two addresses and a mobile number. "I suggest we meet around 11:00 a.m. I am not a morning person as I usually paint well into the early hours."

"I understand. Eleven is fine."

Kessler gestured towards Sam, "I think your presence is being missed?"

Sam was looking over somewhat astonished.

"Ah," Dave said, "I was supposed to be getting drinks!" He hurriedly searched his own wallet for his card, giving it to the artist.

"Here... Kessler handed him two filled wine glasses,

Page 60

"With the compliments of the viticulturist, enjoy!"

Charcoal Gray

Dave's vision barely penetrated the murk. Disorientated, ignorant of his location - he felt helpless. All he knew was that he *must* keep running. The hollow thud, as his trainers pounded the earth, resonated through his ribs. Hot breath licked at his neck, sticky and sweet, bestial and predatory. Hearing the crunch of dry windfall leaves underfoot he guessed he must be in the heart of some dense forest. Darkness loomed, encompassing all trace of scenery, starving his senses, as he ran at full sprint. Then, faintly in the distance he spied a dim beacon, no brighter than a firefly. With a final push of energy, his legs searing, and stitch threatening to rip him within, Dave drew closer. The image pulsed sulphur yellow, the only light - a solitary colour amid a soulless vista. There carved crudely into the bark of an ancient tree was a glowing crucifix.

With a jolt Dave's eyes snapped open, his upper body wrenched his head from its pillow. His brow beaded with sweat; his heart was beating in staccato.

"Dave?" Sam's concerned voice beside him.

"It's ok .... I'm ok ..." he gasped, "Some... stupid nightmare ..." Though his eyes were open and he knew it not to have been real, a trace of the shimmering cross still burned at his retina ...

In preparing for his meeting with Kessler Dave had revisited the information he had stored on his PC, taken some hard copies and zipped them into a soft document wallet. He arrived at the two story converted warehouse in Old Portsmouth dead on eleven as arranged.

Dave pressed the chrome button of the door entry system, spotting the wall mounted CCTV camera above observing him. An audible buzz sounded then Kessler's unmistakable tone.

"Good morning Detective Joseph." A click released the lock. "Come on up."

Dave pushed open the door and entered.

A spacious open planned living area, minimalist in design, formed the ground floor. A chrome and glass staircase stood centre. The ground floor was either used infrequently, Dave thought, or Kessler had a great cleaner. Dave climbed the stairs to the top level. It couldn't have contrasted more. A vast, raised skylight bathed the space with copious natural light, air conditioning keeping the temperature at an even coolness. Kessler stood in front of a large easel, a workbench to his side crammed with artist paraphernalia: scattered sketch books, bottles of turpentine, half squeezed tubes of paint, heavily stained palettes, brushes of all shapes and sizes, and crumpled rags all fought for space. Against the far wall there stood a surgeons stainless steel sink, some kitchen units, a small refrigerator and an industrial coffee machine. A huge side window granted a spectacular view of the Solent, the warehouse having originally provided storage for the port.

Kessler called out from behind his canvas "I bid you welcome, Detective!"

"Thank you," Dave replied "You have quite a view." He gazed out at the horizon, calm summer waters dappled with diamonds of sunlight.

"There is something vital in my spending time by the sea." Kessler said. "And with that space I feel at liberty to imagine without a feeling of containment."

Kessler was dressed in what Dave wondered were pyjamas-silk and loose, oriental in design, blue grey in colour. The look was completed by grey leather sandals and some round, tortoiseshell glasses. It was unconventional attire but Dave had expected nothing less. From where he stood Dave's view of the painting was obscured but he already had familiar goose bumps dotting the surface of his skin.

"Help yourself to coffee." Kessler waved towards the kitchen area, "I am a terrible host- forgive me, please make yourself as if at home. I entertain rarely and have subsequently lost all graces to do so."

Dave made his way to the coffee machine deliberately avoiding looking at the canvas. He felt a need to further prepare for that, the energy transmitted from it was already having a potent effect on his nervous system. He placed his document wallet on the work top. "You want a cup?"

"Thank you - yes, black one sugar, most kind." Kessler replied.

As he fixed the drinks, his back to the artist, Dave raised his voice. "No - thank *you* for agreeing to speak with me. Though I apologise in advance the lack of any structure ... or even ... sense in some of what I say."

"Structure and sense are enemies to the imagination!" Kessler replied, "I insist you ignore them!" He laughed. "Easy for me to say of course, I am not the policeman."

Dave laughed too. He could feel the *energy* boring into the back of his neck from the work-in-progress Kessler original, standing, its paint still wet, only metres away from him. Waves of mixed emotions crescendoed culminating in a sweet torturous anxiety.

Kessler continued, "Though I suppose a detective and an artist are not so divorced from one another? One searches for the truth from many tiny details ... and the other creates their own truth with tiny brushstrokes, both are observers, relating what they see to their particular objective." On hearing no response the artist turned.

Dave was standing motionless staring at the canvas and its composition, mouth open, eyes wide with disbelief- Kessler's brush tipped with Naples Yellow had just painted the image of a *glowing cross on one of a myriad of blackened trees.*

Kessler spoke "Detective Joseph?"

Dave's voice cracked, "I know that place ....." he stammered, "I was there... last night in some dream ... but how?"

"Ah." Kessler removed his glasses. He rubbed his eyes. "So *they* talk with you also?"

"What?" Dave said as if he had misheard.

Kessler fixed him with a probing gaze. "You too are ... *communicated* with?"

Dumbfounded Dave just stared at the painting. "I dreamed it ... the cross ... the trees ... something was chasing me in that forest ... just as you've painted it ..."

Kessler tapped at his temple with the stem of the brush "Just as it was shown to me in here ..."

Dave sat back on the edge of the unit. "What the hell is happening?"

"That ..." Kessler replied, is a very good question!" He approached Dave reaching out for his coffee. "Thank you!"

Dave's hand shook as he lifted the cup, handing it to the artist.

Kessler noticed Dave's tremor, looking analytically from his hand to his eyes. As he took the cup he pointed a slender index finger. "And how long has *that* been going on?"

Dave clenched and unclenched a fist, regaining some control ."Since ... I first started seeing your paintings.....? Not just the originals either, images online - even that bloody label on your wine."

"Ah yes ..." Kessler recalled, "Your fumbling at the exhibition." He smiled.

"It's not just the shaking either, it's ... sweats ... chills, a weird ... glowing around my ribs, a kind of high, a ... euphoria? What does it all mean?" Dave blurted it all out, snatching at breaths, his heart rate noticeably increased.

Kessler in contrast calmly blew his coffee before taking a sip." Where to begin ..." he pondered, "little wonder you sought me out."

"Begin anywhere" Dave replied, "Right now all I have are unanswered questions. If you have any insight on any aspect ... that makes some grain of sense ...?"

"AH, ah!" Kessler interrupted, "We vetoed sense and structure remember?"

Dave threw his palms up in dismay, "If not sense, then what?"

"Theories ... impressions ... abstract thoughts..." Kessler answered, "These are more my domains."

"Then ... share these." Dave urged.

Kessler's gaze was steely. Dave felt like an exhibit being analysed. Kessler spoke, "The artist Chagall once said ... *Painting was like a window ... through which he could have taken flight to another world* ..." Kessler wistfully gestured up at the skylight. "Hmm, my earliest memory is of drawing, I was ... compelled to it, as I am now to paint. It is, for me, an irresistible impulse, obligatory, something over which I possess little or no control. The process itself is... organic...When approaching a work I rarely make preliminary sketches. Instead I enter, one could say, a meditative state and during this time I find myself... *impregnated* with inspiration. Just as you were shown, in your dream, this work before us, I was granted the self-same vision at its conception."

Dave was still sat on the edge of the work top, now sipping at his coffee, silently listening to the artist's words.

"It seems whatever ... force ...that has a hand in my Art has now chosen to open a line of communication with you. The paintings, images are perhaps a link? Through them their originators seem to speak most strongly."

"Their *originators*?" Dave queried.

"Perhaps ...." Kessler replied, "We lack sufficient understanding as to truly know the nature of this source? Perhaps as an artist, dealing in the abstract, the right side of my brain more dominant, thus intuitive, creative, some even speculate psychic; I make a more willing and less questioning subject."

"So why me - my life is all about logic, cold facts and the analysis of them?" Dave said, "Presumably I'm the opposite? Left brain more dominant? And believe me I'm no artist!"

Kessler smiled, "Life cannot just be *logical*, it is also *emotional*, and your job does not define you."

Kessler was right; Dave's early life had been highly emotional. Choosing a career in the Police was probably his way of counter balancing the early trauma, seeking order from chaos.

"You ask *why me*? I think an important question." Kessler continued, "During the last years of his life, Louis Pasteur, the father of modern microbiology, said if he could start over, instead of looking at how the microbe invaded it's host, he would wish to know what it was about a particular host that was so attractive ... He shared your curiosity on such matters.

"You said *Originators*, and earlier you said *they*? Why plural?" Dave's honed listening skills came courtesy of his job.

"Plural? Yes, I believe so," came the reply, "An impression I have ... My work can vary dramatically - some have speculated the paintings could not all have come from the same hand. There is often a noticeable different energy involved. During my periods of meditation I can sense ... changes of character one might say."

"So for instance ..." Dave asked, "The *Salvation* painting in Romania felt very different from say Kate Sinclair's painting?"

Kessler laughed, "I see how your mind is trying to work, Detective Joseph." The artist paused, thinking. "But yes ... The conception of each of those had, a different energy, I would say so yes."

"Once those paintings *moved into the wide world* there were also very different consequences?" Dave observed.

Kessler laughed again, "You are quoting me from my encounter with Miss Nash? Well remembered. Her article, I thought, lacked bite, surprising when one considers how rabid she is?"

It was true. *The Herald* article covering Kessler's appearance at the university was limp and insipid, rehashing the same speculations, adding nothing new.

Dave pressed his point again. "Those two paintings? Dramatic differences in energy and consequence?

"And you overlook..." Kessler answered, "Very different

owners! Another important factor in the equation."

"*The paintings choose their owners*?" Dave queried.

Another laugh, "You rightly use my quotes, to provoke me ... there is I believe a synergy at work, I think like the roots of those trees," he gestured at the image on the canvas, "there is confusion as to where one ends and another begins. Originator, painting, owner - part of a network communicating."

"To what end?" Dave asked.

"Ours is not to reason why?" Kessler mused. "Speaking for myself, it is a successful union. I profit artistically and - yes, economically as a result."

"And what of Kate Sinclair?" Dave asked, "and Mantois, and Levine?"

Kessler met Dave's eyes, betraying no emotion. "I am not immune to their suffering but neither am I responsible for it, no more than the gunsmith is for the murder of one by a bullet. You know this," he held his arms out in front of his body. "This is why you do not snap your cuffs on my wrists and throw me to rot in a cell." He withdrew his arms bringing his cup to his lips.

"I didn't seek you out to arrest you." Dave reassured.

"Then why?"

"To understand," Dave answered, "Both professionally and personally."

"Understand - that those you list caused much hurt in their ... ambition. A lawyer twisting truths choosing profit over justice; a fashion designer, whose Asian workforce, including children, toiled like slaves; an industrialist who's factory's by products threaten to destroy the delicate balance of nature ... Little wonder their actions attracted negative forces?"

"*Their end will be what their actions deserve*?" Dave quoted

Kessler looked at him questioningly.

Dave unzipped his document wallet and removed a print out of the bloody text defacing the painting owned by

Mantois. He held it up for the artist to see. Kessler drew closer, peering through the lenses of round glasses.

"That's the English translation ... the original text is Archaic Latin ... a biblical quote ... found written in Mantois's blood on your painting."

The shocking image seemed more to fascinate and intrigue the artist than repel him.

"Oh," Dave added, "Also, it was written in reverse, a feature I am told attributed to the *demonic*."

"This is my painting?" Kessler asked.

"You can just make out the signature." answered Dave. "See…"

Kessler sighed, then smiled, "The irony is, of course, this painting now is probably priceless, it's ... notoriety will make it infinitely more valuable to some ghoulish collectors."

Dave was surprised by the statement.

Kessler surveyed what lay before him further, "Through his blood ... his DNA ... Mantois has now become one with the painting. True synergy."

Dave felt further surprised and a little creeped out.

"Their end will be what their actions deserve." Kessler repeated, "Pithy." he added.

Dave realised Tybalt Kessler had a very singular viewpoint.

"What have the police made of ... all this?" enquired the artist.

"The official line is a crazed jilted lover or obsessive fan." Dave answered.

"How *unimaginative*," Kessler replied, "but understandable," he paused, "when one considers the *alternative*?"

"Which is?"

"Well …." the artist drained his coffee cup and placed it in the sink, "... that may be something much harder to accept, not something that translates quite so easily into a police report?"

"Go ahead ..." Dave prompted, "I'm listening ... Try me."

Kessler stood by his easel, one hand draped on one corner of the canvas looking at Dave face on. "There are ... *forces* we cannot explain with our ... *science*. The universe is much more ... *exotic* than science would tell us so. There are still many mysteries ... we have theories, but that is all they often are ... just theories. For instance ... in order to make certain mathematic formulas work, in the field of Cosmology, we accept the existence of what we call *Dark Matter*. For every kilogram of Matter five kilograms of this Dark Matter must exist in order to explain the gravity required for our galaxies to move as they do. We are told to ... accept this ... invisible energy's existence, comprised of particles we have not yet the scientific knowhow to detect. Under the banner of *science* we make such a leap of faith."

Dave listened; Kessler's voice was mesmeric, his accent adding a gentle rise and fall.

"Indulge me, further ... on this theme," Kessler said, "in addition to this theory of Dark Matter we are told our universe comprises of *Dark Energy* - an unknown force expanding the universe whilst at the same time filling the void. This ... *nothing* is slowly ... taking over."

An uncomfortable chill travelled the length of Dave's spine. He recalled Professor Naismith recounting of his pursuit by a *Dark, dangerous, malevolent force.*

Kessler spoke again. "If one accepts the existence of *Dark Matter* and *Dark Energy* with no definitive *proof* what other leaps of faith I wonder could one be prepared to take?"

Dave felt light headed, the prolonged exposure to the painting before him, and its euphoric effect, coupled with the strong coffee and Kessler's mind expanding speculations had him reeling within. He was glad for the solidity of the kitchen unit behind him, relieved to be perched on its edge less be fainted to the floor.

Kessler had moved to his work bench, cleaning his brush of the yellow that now imbued the image of the cross carved into one of the nightmarish trees on his canvas. As he worked his voice like a warm molasses quoted from Shakespeare.

"There are more things in Heaven and Earth, than are dreamt in your philosophy…"

Dave's knowledge of the bard was restricted to his school experience - uninspiring. "I'm sorry?" he said

"From Hamlet," Kessler smiled, "and rather apt do you not think?"

"Should I put it in my report?" Dave joked.

Kessler laughed, "You could do a lot worse. For my part I would applaud you." He gathered together some of his tubes of oils and held them up in both hands. "What is it you see?" he asked.

"Paints?" Dave answered tentatively.

"Come closer. More specific!" Kessler thrust the three tubes forward.

Dave left the safety of his perch and approached the workbench. The tubes read: Davy's Grey, Charcoal Grey and Payne's Grey. He smiled, meeting the artist's eye, "Different shades of Grey."

"Yes!" Kessler exclaimed, "You have it! Not all is black or white in our lives, we must accept not everything can be captured and labelled, analysed and easily understood. Why does great Art move us, great music, drama, literature too - how is it we surrender to such artifice our emotions? Is the experience greater for knowing why? Ha - no! *Great forces* exist Detective Joseph, *hidden forces*, just as the force of a lightning bolt striking iron may magnetise it, greater forces may impact on us."

Dave instinctively twirled the bristles of a paintbrush to a point, one amongst many standing in a wooden block. "I accept the existence of such forces, my experiences with your paintings - that dream ... against my better judgement I am forced to ... but it's the intent of these forces that concerns me ... Their capacity for ... evil."

Kessler thought for a moment then spoke. "I understand your concern - I have shared it too ... but the events in Romania, surrounding the orphanage, convinced me otherwise. I have also managed to generate much positive work through my Foundation. Your focus has been on one aspect primarily - do not walk the path of Miss Nash and ignore the whole, preferring to highlight the sensational."

Dave frowned at being compared to the *Herald* reporter.

Kessler continued, "The shades of grey analogy can apply also to *Good* and *Bad* - Aristotle preferred to present us a different concept - *The Mean*. He proposed Good and Bad are not opposites. Good is the *mean* between two bads: excess and deficiency. So ... as an example ... courage is the mean between an excess of rashness and a deficit of cowardice. Using this idea totally transforms our *traditional* view of what may be right or wrong *Grey* becomes good!"

"And Black and White both become bad?" Dave queried.

"Ah." Kessler smiled, "Have I made things worse?" he laughed.

Dave realised he had twirled all the brush heads in the block. "No - it's interesting ... As I told you I had no real expectations about today and besides we banished structure and sense anyway- remember?"

"Yes, yes, wise move on my part!" Kessler said, now stirring his brush in turps.

"Of course I'd like straight forward, clear-cut answers..." Dave continued.

Kessler tutted.

"Okay, okay..." Dave admitted defeat, "But what you've said has confirmed a lot of what I myself have been feeling ... and up to now I haven't really been able to share that, or explore it, so - Thank you."

"And thank *you*," Kessler said, pointing at his block of paintbrushes, "for giving all my brushes bishops mitres!"

Indian Yellow

Early in their relationship Dave Joseph and Sam Paris had agreed Dave would leave his police work firmly at the station gates. The nature of his work often saw him witness to all that was sick in society: lost lives, the shattered, the battered, the corrupt and corrupted. Chewing over the unsavoury details would do nothing for their relationship and drawing a line between the two worlds seemed the solution. But every rule has exception, and for Dave the Sinclair murder and the events in its wake could not easily be locked tight away, rather they bled like ink, through blotting paper, infusing every cell of his being.

More than ever before he was grateful for Sam's presence and, perhaps for the first time, he was seeing and appreciating strengths in her to which he had hitherto been blind. There was something of the *Hippy Chick* in her - she loved those shops that always smelled of joss-sticks, trading jade trinkets, carved Buddhas, yin and yang, bandanas, crystals, incense, and other such wares. She had learned how to perform Reiki healing, believed in the Law of Attraction, and Meditated to calming sounds of nature C.D's. Her art drew from all this and reflected it - often featuring serene natural themes, calm waters, bamboo gently swaying in the breeze, energised sunrises, Zen gardens. Sam was an artist. Sam was spiritual. Surely she would understand.

Before Dave had left Kessler's company the artist had given him a *particularly fine* bottle of rose', sending his warm regards to Sam. On Dave's arrival at home he and Sam had enjoyed a glass talking before, during and after their evening meal. Dave had apologised for *talking shop* but as soon as Sam realised the enormity of the pressure he had been feeling she insisted on knowing everything on his mind.

"It sounds as if Kessler has granted you unique access?" Sam had said over coffee.

"I guess we share some ... kinship? - Both being subject to the same *bizarre visions*." Dave shuddered when he thought of it.

"It's a really thought provoking idea." Sam answered, "Wouldn't *The Prof.* would love all this! Right up his street - *Divine Inspiration!*"

"Yeh." Dave agreed, "Naismith told me - when he felt under attack - walking back from the pub ... he was convinced thinking of that religious painting bought him divine help. His prayers were answered? Art acted as a line of communication?" He laughed, "Like some *cosmic telephone?*" Dave pondered on that thought before shaking his head. "God, listen to me! *Serious Shit.*"

"It's fascinating though..." Sam mused, " we get freaked out about it but our ancestors wouldn't have, they had an innate sense of good and evil...our modern society.... everything is very indistinct, there's a lot of indecision, a *free society* is great but maybe a few more parameters would prevent us from running around like headless chickens quite so much!" Sam embraced the subject with her usual enthusiasm.

"Sometimes..." Dave replied, "I wish it wasn't my job to clear up after our *free society.*"

"You do a lot of good." Sam replied, "And your heart is in the right place... sure you're a typical man - always seeking to *fix* things, but just know you can't *fix* everything. You can't take *great strides* everyday."

Dave smiled.

"I'm not saying Kessler's right," Sam continued, "to be so ... *dismissive* of the lives lost in these cases mixed up and around his paintings, but he has a point about the negative energy they projected into the universe through their abuses? *Like attracts like?* What if the paintings act like some ... great ... amplifier ... hmm ... all Art has a latent power anyway, it's provocative, maybe Art catches us off guard, makes us betray our *true* self in our response to it?" Sam was positively bubbling with unbridled energy.

Dave laughed, "Listen to you! Maybe - I'll lock you, Kessler and *The Prof.* up for a few days and let the lot of you figure it out ... I feel seriously out of my depth in *matters artistic and spiritual*!"

Just then Dave's mobile shook to life on the kitchen counter. Sam being nearest tossed it to him. Congratulating himself on catching it one handed he pressed it to his ear. Dave listened to the distressed voice for a moment and then interrupted, "Whoah....Ok ... Professor, slow down ... Where are you?"

Blue Black

It took Dave a twenty minute drive to reach the archaeology dig site, relying on his *Sat Nav* and garbled directions from the anxious Professor.

Naismith, on guard duty, in his Land rover, had spotted figures - armed with torches, metal detectors and shovels. He had phoned Dave, full of apology, to ask his advice. Dave had instructed him to sit tight and that he would drive out himself whilst also putting in a request for some local uniformed officers to attend the scene ASAP.

Dave parked up, near to the field where the site lay. He grabbed a torch from the glove compartment and pulled his stab vest from the backseat, slipping it on over his t-shirt. Working his way through the undergrowth surrounding the field he located and approached the Land rover tapping on the driver's window. Naismith who was pouring coffee from a thermos flask jumped nervously, sending a splash of hot liquid high from the plastic cup.

Dave mouthed *Sorry* through the window. Naismith, all fingers and thumbs, eventually managed unlocking the door; Dave opened it and leaned in. "Evening Professor."

"Oh Dear boy...Thank you so much for coming - I didn't quite know what else I should do... I do hate to drag you out here though..." Naismith looked tired and agitated.

"No prob. Professor - I've called it in - West Sussex Uniform should be along pretty soon - until then I'm going to get out there and take a look myself - you stay put okay?"

Naismith nodded, his eyes jumped from Dave to the field beyond. "Thank you ... but please, you will be careful?"

Dave closed the car door, checked his torch and made his way into the field.

Other than an impressive full moon in the clear dark sky there was little light. In the distance, however, some small, dancing beams from torches could just be made out. In a half crouch Dave made his way towards them. On leaving home it had been a warm, still, balmy night - but as Dave moved across the uneven terrain the temperature of the air rapidly dropped and a swirling breeze built in its intensity. Dry topsoil started to billow up around him, like cheap cigar smoke, stinging his eyes, catching on his lips. He held his flashlight tightly, the heavy vulcanised rubber of its body solid in his hand. He resisted from switching it on - being alone the element of surprise was his only advantage. Where there had been clear sky now threatening clouds ate at the moon and humidity had turned to rain. The wind whipped droplets into Dave's face. He quickened his pace, feeling the downpour soaking his jeans through to his boxers. Moving in his peripheral vision Dave sensed what felt like a vast shadow pass over him, on looking up more driving rain darted his eyes with cold pins.

Kessler peered at the canvas at the emerging shape of a human figure; pewter lunar key lights barely suggested its form.

A faceless man in a hopeless landscape.

Pelting rain drummed on the roof of Naismith's car; what little vision he had through the windscreen vanished, a constant spatter and wash of film obscuring everything beyond his metal prison. Without thought, he switched on the ignition - seeking the cleansing rhythmic swish of the wipers - unaware, until it was too late, he had also thrown the vehicle headlights on at full beam.

As the extra light from Naismith's car snapped on- Dave heard the *scream.* Swinging the beam towards the source of the sound; his thumb jabbed at the torch switch. He gasped, as his eyes witnessed the surreal scene some distance ahead of him.

A man, in his early twenties, his arms up stretched - one

Page 77

hand clutching a metal detector - was seemingly being *pulled into* the earth. His agonised guttural scream ended as abruptly as it had begun with his head and then arms disappearing through the ground - soil immediately filling the void that remained. It was, Dave thought at that moment, like an old *Bugs Bunny* cartoon he could recall - where carrot tops rapidly descended row by row - accompanied by a whacky sound effect - Bugs craftily purloining a farmer of his crop.

Kessler dabbed delicately at the shadowy figure with his brush.

How is it...he thought..... *a faceless man can scream so loud?*

The alarm of his companion's screams, the car head lights, and Dave's sudden appearance, had the other Night hawker bolting to make his escape.

"Shit." Dave hissed, swinging around his torch, attempting to follow the figure fleeing through a wall of diagonal rain. Bracing his core muscles he pulsed into pursuit. Through the sound of his own heavy breaths and the squeaky thump and slide of his sodden trainers Dave could make out another sound - like that of a loose tarpaulin caught in a gale. His nostrils caught a tang of cordite and once more he sensed a presence shadowing him.

A deafening screech sounded out.

Still running Dave twisted, aiming his torch skyward. In the smallest of moments, no greater than the fast one hundredth of a second of a cameras shutter, Dave's eyes met those of another. But not a humans eyes....piercing, ravenous, primal eyes. With gut wrenching force - a fiery pain at his neck Dave crashed to the ground, swatted aside like a human fly.

Kessler hummed to himself; an old Swedish tune from childhood days. The fine sable point of his brush picked out more tiny details. The painting's desperate figure, dwarfed by monstrous enveloping trees, stood caught like spiders prey. Though featureless, something in the figures stance betrayed he screamed within.

The screams of one lost.... beyond salvation.

What had begun as night time plundering had, for Andy Mullins, turned into a nightmare. The few objects his metal detector had located now rattled in the pockets of his cargo pants as he ran towards the excavation pits at the west side of the field. Rain beat down from a blue black sky, the wind channelling it into his face - mixing with sweat, oily on his brow. With every step he exhaled with a gasp, his mind racing, the desperate scream of his partner in crime echoing in his head like an old scratched record, repeating again and again. Inside he felt fear, a fear he could never have imagined, he recognised the spreading dampness in his cargo pants was not rain. Mullins twisted, trying to locate his pursuer, he could feel its presence, and he could smell it in the air, that Guy Fawkes Night post firework heavy scent. He still gripped his detector in his right hand, the earphones around his neck, spiralling flex connecting man and machine. His army boots thudded at the ground, his gasps more frequent, clothes clinging to him, saturated from within and without.

And then that screech came.

The molars in his mouth, filled with metal amalgam, ached at the sound. It pulled at his guts, hoisting, twisting them upwards, spreading a terror through his whole being. He spun himself round to face whatever stalked him, his boots skidding on the rain soaked dirt. His arms flailing, the detector slipped from his grasp pulling at the earphones around his neck, toppling him off balance. Across his face he felt a searing pain, claws tearing at flesh - revealing bone white beneath. Through pools of red he searched for and found his attackers eyes - *candle bright and unfeeling, intent and soulless.* His legs bucked beneath him, careering him backwards, sending Mullins into one of many excavation pits dotting the field. With a sickening thump, hitting the pit base, his back broke, his precious detector crashing down on top of him. The contents of his pockets scattered, rolling and settling: ancient coins and trinkets embedded once more in the mud from whence they came. Rain hammered down diluting the blood that coursed across his eyes as he stared helplessly upwards. Above him rapidly moving claws propelled loose earth - shovelling it rapidly into the hollow below. Soil stung at Mullins's wounds, flaps of facial skin forced further apart by the weight of the loam. In a last desperate plea the torn almost featureless face started a scream until swallowed earth brought a choking silence.

Dave's breath bubbled at the wet soil, his face turned slightly to one side as he lay on the ground. His eyes flickered, long dark lashes caked in mud. He coughed expelling contents of a puddle he had part ingested. The percussive rain had pooled in his exposed ear - all sound muffled and rippling. A hot lancing pain spread from the left side of his neck, he winced as he felt his shoulder being rocked. He felt himself being turned, rescued from drowning in an inch of water. Half blinking, half squinting he looked up to see Professor Naismith a rainbow of colours surrounding his face, strips of bright colour radiating outwards. Dave smiled weakly then blacked out.

"Over here!" Naismith shouted, waving his torch in his free hand, the other grasping the handle of the large multicoloured golf umbrella he held above his head.

The uniformed police officers ran towards him, blue flashing lights behind them, their patrol car parked by his

Land rover.

"He's breathing..." the Professor informed the nearest officer, ".. But he has a neck wound - lucky I carry a first aid box in the *Rover* - I've stuck a dressing on it ... Poor man's wet through ..."

The officer's colleague talked into his radio, requesting assistance, whilst his partner squatted down beside Dave.

"Maybe while we wait for the ambulance you could tell me what happened?"

As Dave had briefly lost consciousness, having sustained a violent blow to his neck, staff at the Accident and Emergency Department decided to admit him over night. Twenty four hours under observation in the Medical Assessment Unit, assuming there were no complications, was the recommendation.

He now lay comfortably dozing, having been granted a separated room on the ward. A large dressing covered part of the left side of his neck; his chest and shoulders bore several bruises and contusions caused by the body armour as he had impacted with the ground. The stab vest stood by the bedside chair, in which Sam now sat, alongside a *Hospital Property* bin bag containing Dave's sodden clothes.

Sam picked the vest up - a heavy three kilograms - and examined its back. The outer Gortex cover was badly ripped up the left side; the protective Kevlar layers beneath also showed visible damage. An icy pulse crept up Sam's spine as she speculated, but for the vest, the injuries Dave might have sustained. She knew from a previous conversation this type of armour, although referred to as a *stab* vest, was capable also of stopping a bullet in its tracks. Dave had, in a jocular mood, informed her in its testing process - a man would wildly attack it with an ice pick, at which point he had demonstrated his own version of the testing process, and launched at her tickling her frantically. She smiled at the memory, stroking the vest's ripped area, looking down at Dave as he slept. She placed the vest back on the floor and drew her chair close beside him. Closing her eyes she concentrated, clearing her mind of any negative thoughts. She visualized being rooted to the earth - grounded and protected. She brushed her hands down the length of each of her arms, symbolically removing any negative energy. She took a few calming breaths and placed her hands, palms down, over Dave's neck dressing. With slow breaths she visualized *Universal Energy* - a pure, bright, white light beaming down through the crown of her head, coursing through her body, and radiating out through her palms. In her mind where there had been worry now was the desire to heal.

Sarah Nash bit the serrated end from the paper tube sachet containing sugar and poured a steady stream of granules into her foaming cappuccino. Her other hand cradled her phone to her ear as she haunted her usual spot in the *Coffee Bean* café.

"I'm hearing rumours of an incident at the Roman dig site out at Capstan farm?" Nash inquired. She smiled as the denial emerged through the earpiece, "I know it's not your *patch* Sweetie, but that doesn't mean you can't find out for me now does it? Where there's a will there's a way?" She listened to the response, unimpressed, "Well the thing is …." Nash took a sip of coffee froth, "...today is, what we in the newspaper trade call, a *quiet news day,* doesn't happen often, there's usually some grim little soap opera being acted out locally, sordid enough to titillate our loyal readers. But not today, alas. So what one usually finds happening, in a situation such as this, is that journalists turn to … old stories, that for one reason or another, they have suppressed. Usually such stories are withheld to avoid…. scandal, for example: career threatening stories, life wrecking too, potentially, in some cases. Oh, I feel I ought to clarify by explaining it isn't a moral decision withholding publication of these stories. It is usually the case that the subject at the centre of such stories is *useful* to the journalist. Do you understand?"

A familiar rant greeted her ear; she used the time to take a large bite from her oversized chocolate muffin.

"You all finished Sweetie? she finally said, as the rant subsided, "Good - because your protestations are wasting both my time and your own, time that ticks ever closer towards a deadline for publication. And you know... the more I work on this particular *old* story, here on my laptop, the more I realize what a humdinger it is..." Nash's pearly acrylic nails danced over the laptop keys. "So I can expect to hear from you? Good. Sooner is better. Ciao for now!"

Nash turned her attention to the screen in front of her. She smiled as she clicked the *Proceed to checkout* icon, looking longingly at the photograph of the designer handbag. *Come to Mummy.*

Dave's eyes gradually opened, his lashes fluttering as he focussed. He felt the raw sting at his neck and the ache in his shoulders, chest, and ribs. Seated by his bed, curled up in the armchair Sam stirred.

Trying to speak Dave croaked, he cleared his throat, trying again. "Hello Wombat."

Sam yawned and stretched, her eyes smiling.

"You been here all night?" Dave asked.

"Got here as soon as Naismith called me. Don't you remember? I was down in A& E with you."

Dave raised his eyebrows, "Hmm... don't seem to remember," he attempted to sit up, provoking a sharp intake of breath.

"You're suffering concussion ... hold on ... just relax back," Sam used the beds remote to incline it behind Dave's head. "How's that? Better?"

Dave rested back into the pillow, "Yeh - thanks, how about a kiss?"

Sam leaned and kissed him softly "How you feeling? You had me worried. What the Hell did this to you?"

"Honestly? I have no idea. I caught a glimpse but.....*what* it was - I don't know..... but I'm okay, you mustn't worry. You know I'm a tough old rooster! I'm just a little sore around the edges that's all, Shit love, what have I got myself into?" He felt at the neck dressing, "Ouch."

"Don't fiddle!" Sam rebuked. "And try not to think about things, you have to rest."

"So, are we going to play nurses and patients? That would take my mind of things!"

"You wish!" Sam plumped his pillow, and kissed his nose, "You just rest."

Dave grinned, "You were watching me sleep weren't you?"

"Sure." Sam sat back down.

"I remember you told me you liked watching me sleep when we first started seeing each other. I thought it was kinda sweet, a little weird, but sweet – Thanks for staying with me... through the night. Good knowing you were here!"

"Where else would I be NumbNuts?" She took his hand and kissed it.

Dave raised her hand to his mouth and kissed it back. "Thanks anyway." He looked at the door "You think they've forgotten breakfast?"

Sam's eyes rolled, "Shall I go find out Greedy Guts?"

All hopes of an uninterrupted recuperation evaporated at lunchtime with the appearance of D.I. Leighton bedside.

"Thought I'd dispense with the grapes. They only give you the shits anyway." he bellowed, wheeling the meal table away, with Dave's half eaten lunch still on it. He nodded a brief acknowledgement Sam's way, noting her displeasure, and then tossed a file in Dave's lap. "Sorry to bother you, being on your death bed and all, but I have to shoot off next couple of days to the Smoke, some bloody course on *Improved interviewing of suspect* or some such namby pamby bullshit. Still, overnight stay in a hotel in the centre of London's a pleasant change of scenery. Anyhow, I won't be around so need to grab you now seeing as how you'll be taking the reins again. God help us all."

Dave opened the file and looked through its contents:

photographs and a report on the two murders at the dig site.

Leighton continued, "Our colleagues over at West Sussex Constabulary are keen for us to play an active role in the investigation, bearing in mind some similarities to the Sinclair murder, and your direct involvement. Why the bloody hell you were out there, in the middle of the night, unofficially, in the first place search me. However, the impression seems to be it's your bloody mess and you can clear it up."

Sam threw Leighton a cross look.

Dave, sensing her irritation, turned to her, "Hey Sam why don't you take a break for a few - grab a coffee. We won't be long."

"Okay.." Sam got up and made for the door, "You are supposed to be resting though."

"I know and I will, I promise. Let me just go through this." Dave winked.

With Sam having vacated her seat, Leighton collapsed into it. "They'll need a full statement from you of course, officers at the scene got little sense from you after you came round, your pal Naismith filled in the rest."

"Not sure what to report - it was dark, I remember snatches, but even those seem bizarre. The concussion perhaps?" Dave's mouth tightened as he saw photos of the two recovered bodies: Mullins face like a peeled banana, skin pulled aside, revealing globular eyes, ivory teeth, the other corpse with dirt impacted in his screaming mouth, caking his features and hair.

"Funny thing is," Leighton pointed to the photo, "Archaeologists have been searching that site for months, with little to show for it. Our Scenes Of Crime boys dig him out of the ground and in the process uncover some vast Roman mosaic floor! They think there are remains of a palace under there."

"Really..." Dave pondered, "Strange shit keeps happening ..."

Leighton was examining the damaged stab vest. "Fuck

me … what the hell did this?"

"I don't know Guv!" Dave said, examining the photos, "but it did for these two - one thing I'm sure of; it wasn't human."

Leighton sighed, "Don't tell me…let me guess….something capable of inflicting *injuries more consistent with an attack on the plains of Africa*?"

Dave was shaking his head, "*Africa*? No….. I don't think Africa is where it came from…."

Shortly after Leighton's visit Dave was discharged from the hospital. D.C. Sunderland had kindly retrieved Dave's car from the dig site, he had further offered to drive Dave and Sam home. A large, hurriedly wrapped, gift package now sat on the backseat in between them.

"For you Sarge…a little present from the boys and girls in the office." Sunderland grinned, looking at the couple through his rear view mirror.

"You shouldn't have..." Dave said as tore at the paper.

"Don't get too excited!" Sunderland laughed.

Dave smiled as the contents became revealed, "Very funny…" - the bulk of the package comprised of a new stab vest, but attached to its rear hung a soft toy - a fluffy bat complete with oversized vampire teeth. He shook it, its wings flapping, turned it, and showed Sam.

She laughed and stroked its domed head, "Cute – I'll call it *Boris*!"

Dave attempted to raise his lolling head, his heavy eyelids coaxed open by the spreading sensation of heat traversing his face and body. Senses dulled by deep sleep gradually became more aware – like a plane emerging from an electrical storm having been forced to fly blind. The horizon was spinning, the landscape slowly revolving then disappearing altogether. Dave blinked several times, gulped as his throat rasped dry. The heat intensified, in his nostrils hung a familiar scent - one of … cooking…roasting. Plumes of smoke stung at his eyes but wanting to rub them he was somehow unable. A sudden realisation: his arms were fastened behind his back, his legs too, wrists and ankles tied, securing him to the giant spit slowly turning, suspended over flaming coals. The smell was his own – not the oozing fat and crisp crackling of a hog – but his own parched skin, stretched and seared. The full horror dawned on him and deep from his belly he screamed.

The bedside lamp crashed from the night table, scattering glass and ceramic as Dave's arms thrashed wildly. His breathing was loud and rapid, his chest heaved, sweat oozed from every pore. Rapidly switching her side lamp on, Sam clutched at Dave's flinching torso, comforting him, calming him; she soothed his brow with kisses, talking to him softly. Dave's panic subsided, normality gradually returned; he stared blankly at the ornate plaster ceiling rose above, unable to speak, his body still prickling with heat from an open fire.

Transparent Yellow

Though not feeling a hundred per cent, Dave felt returning to work and resuming the investigation was the best therapy. Sam had shown considerable concern at his disturbed night but respected his decision. He had removed his neck dressing that morning. What lay beneath were three semi healed gashes - raised and red, likely scar bearing he had been informed at the hospital. They tingled, as if mild electric shocks ran over the tissue surface; the whole area felt on fire. Conveniently his shirt collar hid most of damage. Whatever had taken a swipe at him had merely glanced his back and neck; he had not felt its full force. Others at the site had not been so fortunate. Dave had to wonder why he had been spared, taking into account the brutal nature of the beast involved. He certainly didn't consider he owed his life to his body armour, if that *creature* had really wanted him dead he felt sure twenty eight layers of Kevlar would not have stood in its way.

Dave parked up and made for the Police Station entrance.

"What the fuck's going on?" Dave said, as he saw the swarm of suited figures in the outer office, noticing two more in the office shared by him and Leighton.

D.C. Sunderland called from behind his desk "*Professional Standards Unit* Sarge."

"*What?*" Dave glanced around as the suited strangers busily accessed computers and searched through file cabinets.

Sunderland continued, "The Chief Super is foaming at the mouth – you not seen *The Herald* today? We got ourselves another leak and word from up high says heads will roll this time ... welcome back Sarge!"

"For fucks sake ...." Dave squared his shoulders and marched to his office.

"Here Sarge ... catch," Sunderland tossed Dave his copy of *The Herald* "*You made the papers!*"

Dave caught it and read the headline

"*Cursed archaeological site claims victims.*"

"Why the fuck does everything have to be cursed in Sarah Nash's world? Jesus." He continued reading as he entered his office. He greeted the two officers rooting through case files. "Do whatever you have to guys; just let me get to my desk ok?"

It wasn't long before Dave received a summons from D.C.S. Steele, and he found himself facing the Chief Super in grave mood.

"You've seen the headlines then?" Steele pointed to the paper Dave carried.

"Yes sir, another Nash hatchet job - though, now I've read it I can see why Professional Standards have become involved, the bodies weren't even cold and Nash has got all the info. Has to be a direct leak."

"Indeed." Steele replied "There is…considerable pressure to isolate and eliminate the source of the leak. You, more than anyone, have been privy to every aspect of the investigations Miss Nash has reported on. Therefore, I am duty bound to ask you some searching and direct questions-whilst supporting Professional Standards in thoroughly examining your working practices. Do you understand D.S. Joseph?"

"Of course Sir and I will cooperate fully. I have nothing to hide and importantly nothing to *gain* from leaking details to *The Herald*. We spoke previously on how unusual these cases have been, having their details splashed across the pages of *The Herald* can only compromise any attempt towards a serious investigation."

Steele nodded; he seemed to appreciate the words. Returning to the papers headline he asked, "What do you make of this latest article? You're mentioned this time by name."

"Well… as usual Nash goes for the sensational, choosing *this time* to focus on notions of the site being *haunted… cursed* - she mention Professor Naismith and my being there

- of course that gives her an excuse to make a tenuous link to Kessler through Naismith and the university. I seem to be blamed somewhat for not preventing the two men's deaths.."

"Do you share that opinion?" Steele asked, fixing his gaze.

"No sir, I do not." Dave answered, "I'm just fortunate I didn't join them. I don't think *anyone* could've stopped what happened."

Steele sighed "I have read the reports. Again we are faced with an unconventional adversary....So... what in your opinion could be responsible?"

"Honestly sir? I don't know. But I am committed to find out. None of this has remotely diminished my resolve to uncover the truth." Dave glanced down at the paper, "Sir, one thing I do find odd about this article ..."

"Oh?" Steele's chin rose.

"Nash stresses my being involved in the Sinclair murder investigation, and my interviewing Kessler, but she neglects to mention D.I. Leighton is heading up the case."

Steele moved uncomfortably in his chair, "Your point D.S. Joseph?"

Dave tapped at the headline, "The reality of the situation is, yes, largely I have been directing these investigations, you know yourself the D.I. has shown little support, but only you, I, and Leighton know that. Officially it's Leighton's show. I'd expect to see at least a mention of the D.I. in charge, wouldn't you Sir?"

Steele sighed, picking up the paper to reread it. "I really hope you're wrong on this..."

On returning from the meeting with Steele, Dave was stopped by D.C. Sunderland in the outer office.

"How did it go Sarge?"

"Ok thanks, we are just going to have to be patient and put up with some serious nosing around in our business for a while."

"Just as well Leighton's not here, he'd be going ballistic,"

Sunderland grinned.

Dave looked through the doorway into his and Leighton's office, an officer was sat in front of the D.I.'s computer.

"Yeh, trust him to miss out on all the fun."

Sunderland laughed, "A course trying to teach *him* the *subtleties of interview technique*? Good luck to them on that one!"

"Amen to that! I miss anything - while I was gone?" Dave asked.

Sunderland snapped his fingers, "Almost forgot Sarge, some bloke asking for you at reception, been here about half an hour."

Dave shrugged, "Who is he? What's he want?"

Sunderland searched his desk, cluttered with papers.

"Christ!" Dave remarked, "Look at the state of your desk! Professional Standards gonna have a field day with you!"

"Ha Ha.." Sunderland answered, "I have my *own* system … ah here it is," he pulled a pink Post-it from the confusion, "the guys name is *Stamp* - he's from some *monastery*? He's here because he read the paper, thinks he might be able to help."

Dave sighed "Are you taking the bloody piss?"

"No Sarge, honest to God, he's down at the front desk now."

"That's just what I need – a bloody crackpot monk stalking me."

Approaching reception Dave saw *him* - sat on one of the blue plastic wall mounted seats facing the enquiry desk. He clearly wasn't the monk Dave had been expecting.

Stamp looked in his mid twenties, about 5ft 8in tall and extremely well exercised. His hair was brown, short, and somewhat uncontrollable in its tousled nature; his clothes were well worn but clean: black jeans, a white t-shirt and black Converse baseball boots heavily scuffed. If anything he looked less like a monk and more like a skateboarder. On a seat beside him stood a small dark rucksack.

Page 91

The threat posed by terrorism made strangers with rucksacks particular figures of suspicion, Dave therefore eyed him cautiously as he drew closer. And then ...Dave spotted it.....running the entire length of the man's right forearm... Dave saw the cross; a large tattooed, shaded design in black ink. A heaving sensation hauled Dave's gut... *Another cross*?

"Mr Stamp?" Dave composed himself.

The man smiled, rose from his seat and extended his hand, "Yes, *Finlay* Stamp."

"I'm Detective Sgt. Joseph - I believe you asked to see me? In relation to the current murder investigations?" Dave shook Stamps hand, eyes drawn to the flexing tattoo. "You think you may be of some assistance?"

"I may be, yes," Stamps voice was surprisingly cultured, at odds with his appearance, "That's to say; my services are at your disposal."

Dave tilted his head slightly, "And what *services* are these exactly?"

"I'm a Demonologist." Stamp said, as casually as one might say they were a newsagent, "and it's my belief that your murderer is a demon...."

After a brief, stunned silence Dave suggested Stamp and he continue their conversation in one of the more private interview rooms. In previous circumstances Dave would have dismissed Stamp as a crank and sent him packing, but recent events had propelled him to search deeper and wider in his quest for the truth. In any case with Professional Standards crawling everywhere Dave had little chance of achieving much in the office. There was something else too, an odd sense of...*relief*? This rucksack carrying, tattooed stranger had in the matter of a few words claimed what Dave had dared not. Sure, he and Professor Naismith had danced around the idea of the supernatural being involved, but coming right out and saying the murderer was a demon? Stamp had balls; he had to give him that.

Dave scratched at the hair on his crown, realising he was baffled as to how to proceed.

Stamp broke the tension, gazing around the sterile room, "I've never been in a police interview room before."

"Glad to hear it!" Dave sat opposite him, "Right now it's the quietest place available, don't let it intimidate you."

"Actually, I don't get intimidated." came Stamps unexpected reply. I'm incapable of experiencing it - I have a rare form of Autism apparently, and like several other emotional responses intimidation is something foreign to me. I've never felt it ... not even as a boy - the monks said I was a *kamikaze toddler* - totally fearless." He laughed, "I think I must have been a worry!"

"Monks?" Dave queried.

"Yes. I was brought up in a monastery, that's where I still live, in Almouth. *Legend* has it I was abandoned on the steps as a baby. The monks saw me as a *gift from God*, and it was eventually agreed, after much bureaucracy, they could raise me. I was lucky my mother chose their door. Thanks to the monks' devotion I had a charmed upbringing."

Dave raised both eyebrows. That explains the cross, he thought, his eyes falling on the tattoo once more.

Stamp spoke further, "You probably think I've been hammered with religious doctrine all my life? Far from it, the brothers and the Abbot all came from very different backgrounds, varied walks in life, a real cross section. Deeply spiritual men yes, but warm, funny intelligent and nurturing too. They all, in their way, have contributed toward the making of the man I am today - I have been spoilt for mentors! And as for the *cross*, I see it has caught your eye ..." Finlay held his hand palm up displaying his forearm, "That is simply protection."

"As a ... *Demonologist*? " Dave asked.

"Yes."Stamp answered.

"Forgive me..." Dave paused, "What exactly is a demonologist?"

Finlay sat back in his chair, "In essence: someone who

endeavours to protect those threatened physically and or mentally by demonic phenomenon, should this prove beyond the demonologists capability then the matter may well fall to the realm of the church and the exorcist. You're probably more familiar with that side?" Stamp delivered the explanation in the same casual manner as he had first introduced himself.

"Only through movies…" came Dave's response.

"Ah, well that won't get you very far! How well do you know your bible?" Stamp enquired.

"If I said I was rusty that would be an understatement!"

"I'm not here to sell it! But it's a good read!" Stamp smiled, "Give it a go sometime. Well, in both testaments angels and demons are mentioned some three thousand times. And if that whets your appetite, there's Michael Psellus and his eleventh century volume *The Classification of Demons*. And if you think it's all *ancient* history I can tell you that even now at pontifical universities in Rome demonology is taught alongside philosophy, theology, psychology and anthropology. All major religions have dedicated clergy specialising in demonology."

Dave's eyebrows lifted again, "I had no idea."

"Most monasteries were originally funded by rich patrons, the monks' prayers an insurance policy against Satan and damnation. In the world I inhabit these matters are daily concerns. Fortunately it is rare these days that outside forces directly impact on people's lives, but when they do - they are hell bent on destruction - the results can be devastating."

"And you think these … *demonic forces* are responsible for the recent murders?" Dave asked.

"Once one has hacked through Sarah Nash's rhetoric; it seems a likely conclusion." Stamp replied, "Of course if I could be granted access to more reliable sources of information?"

"With respect," Dave answered, "You could be on Sarah Nash's payroll."

"With equal respect, so could you." Stamp replied, "I heard the desk sergeant mention the Professional Standards Unit overrunning the building. Putting two and two together I'd guess your department has a leak?"

Dave clenched his jaw, "That, as you must be aware, is a police matter."

"Of course." Finlay smiled, "I appreciate your position. I came here today to offer my assistance; whether you choose to accept it, on whatever level - it's your call. I am happy to speak in generalities, if that is your wish? Just know you are not alone in your endeavours…visit us at Almouth Monastery; Abbot Michael is a font of knowledge." Stamp unzipped a section of his rucksack, drawing out a flyer - inviting visitors to the retreat - he also pulled out a biro and scrawled on the flyers rear. "This is my mobile number. " Stamp peered up from his writing. "Do you like honey Detective?"

"Uh, yes?"

"I ask because we keep bees. I promise you it is the best honey you can imagine. And forget all the over processed crap you see in the supermarket; this is the proper stuff, raw and unfiltered. "

"I'll remember that," Dave took the flyer. "Thank you."

Finlay replaced his pen in its zipped compartment. Nonchalantly he said "That wound on your neck, burns I imagine?"

Dave touched at it, feeling the electric shock sensation buzzing at his skin. "Like the mother of all razor burn," he replied.

Stamp stood, and in one smooth movement removed his t shirt. His body was taut and muscled with strongly defined abdominals usually only seen on cover models in fitness magazines. He turned to reveal a trio of scars lining his upper back and left shoulder. "They still give me restless nights…even now." The scars made Dave's neck wounds pale into insignificance,

"How did you get them?"

Stamp slipped his shirt back on. "Same way as you got yours I imagine. I got in the way of a *Soul Feaster*."

Dave's head noticeably jerked backwards "A *Soul Feaster*?"

"A low order *demonic entity*."

"*Low order*?" Dave realised his mouth gaped open like that of a goldfish.

"A Soul Feaster is a…debased, bestial entity with limited knowledge and intellect, low ranking in the diabolical hierarchy - it terrorises, kills and feeds on the souls it claims. Does that sound anything like your killer?"

Dave had to admit it did, "You can appreciate it isn't easy for me to … take such a… *leap*?"

Stamp shrugged, "Easier to deny such a thing exists, but do you have a suitable alternative explanation?"

"As a policeman I feel it is my duty to explore *all* possibilities." Dave answered, "I am interested in what you have to say Mr Stamp, but you'll understand it is….*new territory*, and I need to remain objective."

Stamp gently rocked his head from side to side, "I hear you - and please call me *Fin*. No one calls me Mister Stamp, maybe a Doctor might have … a Bank Manager maybe, oh and a Driving Examiner but that's it…."

"Okay." Dave smiled; he liked Stamp's unusual manner. "You talked of a hierarchy?"

Stamp nodded, "There are plenty of published references like *Psellus* classifying orders of demons, but simply put: there are low order entities like the Soul Feaster, whose methods are brutal, their objectives simple, and higher forms, shrewder, more calculating, more knowledgeable, with their own agendas. On rare occasions these orders work together, behind the brutality of the Soul Feaster a higher order entity plots - When this occurs…things get *really* ugly!"

Dave felt his neck hairs rise, accompanied by an unwelcome cold caress down his spine. "What kind of *agendas* are we talking about?"

Finlay paused before answering, "Mans soul belongs to

God, to attack and steal that soul withholds it from God. It lays down a challenge. Demonic entities are jealous of mans incarnate form; this spurs them to desecrate the body and blood. Added to this, let us not forget Hell is intolerable, and not just to man - demons also torment *one another*. Terrorising and possessing man on earth brings temporary escape from these torments. In its widest sense the diabolic hierarchies main goal is to seek mans ruination and to seize Earth in front of the eyes of God."

Dave listened to Stamps cultured voice, his tone and phrasing were not melodramatic though Christ knows the subject matter would warrant it. He spoke as someone with direct experience of his topic, the scars on his back were evidence too he was not merely speculating.

Finlay continued, "There is, if you like, a battle being waged, in the divide between life and death, the world as we know it and that which lies beyond. A battle, that at its heart, has mans soul as its prize. For the most part, it is a war to which we are totally oblivious, but on occasion it spills over into our own experience and these forces of good and evil gain access to our world."

As Dave listened he was reminded of something Kessler had said…a quote mentioning a window to another world. At that moment he would have loved to tell Stamp everything…about Kessler, the paintings, the Mantois text, his parents…but he dare not, at least, not yet, perhaps with D.C.S. Steele's authorisation, but how in Gods name would he convince the Chief Super he hadn't gone barking mad with talk of … demons, soul feasters …

"I can see I have given you much to think on?" Stamp broke Dave's thoughts. "I'm sure it is a lot to take in - judging by your neck you've already had direct experience of it. May I ask you, as a child, were you baptised?"

Dave answered taken aback somewhat, "Yes … I was."

"Good." Stamp answered, "That will help. Baptism is a form of exorcism, not many realise its origins."

Dave sat back, "You are full of surprises Mr…" he

corrected himself, "*Fin*."

Finlay shrugged, "My particular strain of Autism makes me direct, and my upbringing has been unconventional, under the tutorage of men who have chosen to serve God. From an early age I took a keen, some may say, *obsessive* interest in historical recordings of, and references to, demonic attacks and possessions. I was always bursting with questions and thirsty for knowledge! I found my calling - not as a monk - but in a different way: serving in Gods army - to fight evil. I sought out exorcists and requested to learn from them, accompanying and assisting them in their work. I have fought on the front line of this, the oldest of wars. I know the risks are great, the threats ever present, but these things unconcern me. My lack of fear makes me an ideal candidate to be a demonologist. A few knocks and scars won't deter me… how about you? Are u deterred by what has happened, by what I have shared with you?" Stamp ended his speech with a wide smile.

"All in the line of duty!" Dave replied, "Listen, you're right - you have given me a lot to think over. Right now my hands are tied. I can't discuss details and I am mindful of not wishing to add further to disclosures of sensitive material. Let me mull everything over, take stock, speak to my superior - I will also be checking up on you; it's only fair to warn you of that."

"No problem." Stamp answered, "Try to visit Almouth, if you can - you have my number."

"Thank you, yes." Dave folded the flyer and pocketed it. He stood, Stamp joining him, "I'll see you of the premises."

As Stamp grabbed his rucksack Dave's eyes once more settled on the black shaded cross.

Mars Black

London. The Prince Regent Hotel approaching midnight. D.I.
Leighton had tumbled from the black cab, heavily reeking of
scotch. Fellow police attendees at the *Improved Interviewing
Techniques* seminar and he had hit the pub once their training
had ended and made a boozy night of it. In Leighton's words
the seminar was *A waste of bloody time - psychobabble
pandering to the civil liberties brigade* and he added *Soon
we'll be so bloody powerless they may as well castrate us,
and shove our balls up our arses.* Having tipped the cabbie
Leighton wrestled with the revolving door to the hotel, his
jacket snagging in the join between the door and rubber seal
momentarily yanking him backwards.

"Shit." he examined his torn jacket pocket. "Twenty five
fucking years I've had this suit." The suit in question hadn't
been fashionable on purchase and looked charity shop
material now. A shade of brown that resembled tobacco,
Leighton's reason for choosing it; it wouldn't show the dirt.
Muttering he collected his key from reception and took the
elevator to the top floor. With a cheery *ping* the doors
opened, and Leighton lurched from the lift. He muttered
some more on viewing the non smoking signs plastering the
corridor. His hands frisked at his pockets finding his mobile
rather than the *Dunhill* he sought. "Shit." Realising he had
not switched his phone back on after the days training, he
stabbed at its power button. The screen glowed to life.
Leighton's blood shot eyes narrowed as he tried to focus - the
signal strength, indicator barely registered, "Arse!" Leighton
looked back at the elevator and then noticed the stairwell
with a sign arrowed *To roof.* "Where else would it fucking
lead? Heaven? Hmphh." He began frisking his pockets again,
as he ascended the stairs.

By the time Leighton emerged out onto the roof he had a
king-size hanging from his mouth, bobbing as he puffed from
his climb. He took a suck as his hand shielded the cheap
throwaway lighter; his cigarette sparked orange at the tip.

Taking a long draw he sighed, exhaling a puff of rolling smoke. He peered at his mobile's screen, the signal now up to full strength. Leighton pressed the phone to his ear, listening on voicemail to his missed calls. "Shit." the word escaped like a hiss of gas. His eyes darted as he listened. His finger jabbed at the number pad, forwarding to another message, and then another. He pulled in a lungful of smoke, holding it deep then slowly let it escape from his nose.

The view was wasted on Leighton. London by night; multicoloured lights danced like those at Christmas, familiar landmarks silhouetted against a Mars Black sky.

A city alive.

Kessler sat on the brown leather sofa in the lower level of his studio warehouse; his knees drawn up they supported a large sketch pad, in his right hand a length of charcoal. On the armrest beside him lay some correspondence. He had been commissioned to design a poster for The Swedish National Ballet's forthcoming production *Ophelia*. He had been sat in the dark for an hour - meditating, emptying his mind, tuning in and finally receiving, hardly moving in body but his mind infusing with ideas, as *The Originators* locked onto his wavelength. Now it was time to translate these transmissions... to grant them life.

Still clutching his phone, Leighton scuffed at the tarmac, a few loose stones chipping across the roof surface. He gazed upwards as he smoked. His eyes now had a trace of resignation in them, a bellyful of scotch helping nullify his reactions. He was close enough to the roof edge now to peer over, the dizzying height risked him regurgitating the evening's liquor, and he swallowed hard. Coldness caught him unawares; he pulled at his jacket collar performing a little shimmy to encourage circulation, the temperature was definitely falling, and quickly.

The charcoal broke with a biscuit snap as Kessler's hand darted across the landscape orientated sketch book. He continued - using the remaining black stump - blacking in elements of his composition: A black stream, a precarious hanging willow with its leaves dipping at the water, a blossom tree - its flowers tumbling in the breeze, the figure of Ophelia sat on the bank, feet submerged in the inky water, in her hands a clutched posy.

A chilling fog veiled Leighton's view, the city lights like a child's kaleidoscope spied through a cataract. Clouds had gathered too, swirling, shifting across the night sky. The D.I. puffed on his second cigarette, still clutching at his phone, occasionally casting it an anxious glance. Then, with ferocious volume, seemingly from nowhere, like the sudden arrival of a low flying plane, came the strangled screech. Leighton spun round to see the shadowy form; simultaneously his face was ripped from his head.

Ophelia's gaze stared deep into the dark waters - drawn by the gentle, winding current. The swaying rushes on the opposite bank beckoned her forwards. Her gossamer gown, diaphanous in the early morning sun, clung to her slender form, cupping her breasts, hugging her hips, the neckline low and pulled open. Her right hand plucked at the petals of the blooms she delicately cradled; tiny leaves settled on the rivers gloomy film.

Blood spurted in geysers, as facial nerves shredded, Leighton's screaming his last utterance on the planet. His worn dessert boots slid and scraped on the roofs gritty surface, his body recoiling backwards from another strike. The creatures talons tore at his features, pulling the skin away like parchment from a disintegrating book, a seething mass of butcher block red remaining. Still grasping his phone Leighton raised his arms in futile defence, his thumb searching blindly for the smooth raised metal button. The pad of his thumb located its raised goal. He raised the mobile to where once he had owned a face. The exaggerated digital click of the phones camera mimicked the shutter of a much older device. He pressed again - another click. The suede of his once fawn boots was now stained red, the fibres fat and sodden. Another thunderous strike and Leighton's heels traversed the roof's edge, his upper body reeling, arms flailing. As his soles desperately searched for solid ground, with the lurching momentum of falling backwards, through one remaining eye, pooled scarlet, Leighton saw the beasts returning stare - an expression of both hate and hunger. As D.I. Leighton plummeted through London's night sky on the roof, high above, a half smoked cigarette, still lit, rolled in perfect revolutions tumbling from the edge until with a fading grace it finally extinguished.

Olive Green

The ringtones bleating dragged Dave begrudgingly from his slumber. He pawed at the night table eventually finding his phones smooth casing and dragged it towards him. He answered, eyes still half shut. The grim tone of D.C.S. Steele. D.I. Leighton was dead.

"I can appreciate what a shock this must be," D.C.S Steele sorted through some papers, "You worked closely with the man for a year and a half after all."

Dave's eyebrows were raised, not only was Leighton dead but Professional Standards had identified him as the leak; their investigations had further uncovered evidence pointing towards corruption. The whole thing was incredibly sad and added to the mixed emotions Dave was already feeling. "It's certainly a lot to take in." Dave admitted, "What info have you got on his death sir?"

"Well, I had a long phone conversation with my opposite number in London early this morning; the pathologist is on the case as we speak. I was told, however, that although he clearly fell from the hotel roof Leighton had already sustained significant injuries prior to this." Steele quoted from his notes. "*Deep lacerations to face, consistent with attack from large clawed animal...*"

Dave rubbed at the back of his head. "Oh Jesus…" the wound on his neck felt a tingle ripple through it.

"Indeed…." Steele responded, "You can see now why I was so eager to speak to you in person? I've asked to be informed immediately as to any developments."

"Are we certain he was Nash's source?" Dave asked.

"A pretty clear picture is emerging. One look at his mobile phone records shows communication between them escalating during periods of leaked information." Steele sighed, "This, and proven links to known felons, suggesting Leighton's conspiring in keeping them from the reach of the law, contribute towards a not inconsiderable and regrettable stain on his character."

"Hmm.... some epitaph." Dave commented. Leighton had been testing to work with, but he had taught Dave a lot, and for better or worse he had been one of a dying breed.

Steele could sense Dave's introspection. "For what it's worth, D.S. Joseph, D.I. Leighton liked you very much, and respected you as a police officer."

A half laugh escaped from Dave's nose, "You think?"

"You, better than most, know the type of man he was, one had to...*read between the lines*, navigate his brusqueness, he thought you a good D.S., supportive and efficient and with definite D.I. potential...as do I."

"Thank you Sir." Dave answered, "I hope you still feel the same way as this investigation continues. I think it will test us all considerably and, if handled poorly, risks bringing us a truckload of negative attention."

Steele smiled, "Many moons ago, I sat where you are now...in that seat...a young D.S. trying to get *everything* right... attempting to please *everybody*... I have faced many challenges in my career; most I have succeeded in overcoming, hence my sitting this side of the desk today! Time I hope has made me a little wiser and accepting, aware of my own and others limitations. There is no...*perfect formula* for success...trial and error plays a part... instincts too. In our work we must rely on our dogged determination...be like the proverbial *bloodhound* - sniffing for a scent, following its trail...to wherever it may lead. Keep going D.S. Joseph, keep the momentum moving forward and push onwards, some days movement will be slight, other days you will take giant strides and achieve progress and a deeper understanding. I have total faith in your abilities, and that is why, with no resources to replace D.I. Leighton presently and the inevitable aftermath of what Professional Standards have unearthed, you must for now, head up this case and continue following this trail under your own volition. You shall, of course, have my unwavering support; my office door is always open. I have every confidence in your ability to fathom what we are dealing with…" Steele widened his eyes, *"claws and all."*

"Thank you Sir. I will endeavour to live up to your expectations." A knock at the door halted Dave's reply.

"Come in," Steele beckoned.

The desk sergeant entered with a large padded envelope, "Sir, this arrived by courier for you."

"Thank you."

Steele took the packet and started opening it as the sergeant left. "Ah…" Steele uttered, "D.I. Leighton's personal effects."

Dave watched as the D.C.S. emptied the contents on the surface of his desk: a wallet, wristwatch, cigarette packet, plastic lighter and Leighton's mobile its screen badly cracked. "Did they check his phone?" Dave asked.

Steele attempted to power it up "Broken it would appear?"

"May I sir?" Dave held out his hand. Steele passed it to him. Dave examined it, removing its back casing, adjusting the battery. Still the screen remained dead.

"Of course we can check with the network on any calls made or received. Professional Standards were already collating that information." Steele said.

"Did it fall with him from the roof? Surprised it's so intact." Dave asked.

Steele consulted his notes, "Uhhhhm…No .It was discovered on the hotel roof, found when crime scene officers did a thorough sweep."

Dave bit his top lip deep in thought. "So the D.I. was *using* it? - *Before* he fell? It clearly wasn't in his pocket?"

"No. Apparently not." Steele thumbed through his transcript of his earlier conversation with the D.C.S in London.

"Like I said…It's still pretty intact." Dave removed the back plate again, "The lab will probably be able to retrieve anything stored." he removed the MicroSD Memory Card, "Nothing wrong with that," Dave's brow furrowed "What do the call logs show from the mobile provider - anything around the time of death?"

Steele scanned his records, "Time of death around midnight...No calls at all...although Nash had left him two voicemails... they were made earlier in the day, warning him about Professional Standards I bet. I hazard a guess she would have known they were on the case."

Dave continued, "Ok. So he wasn't making a call then," Dave paused, he held the phone out in front of him, in his mind recreating Leighton's possible last actions. "I wonder..."

"What?" Steele moved forwards in his chair.

"In those circumstances..? Hmm a long shot...but a copper with that much experience.... just maybe...where's the camera on this thing?" Dave searched and found the smooth, raised, metal button. "Sir, can you get someone to bring a memory card reader in here?"

Minutes later D.C. Sunderland knocked and entered with the hardware requested. Dave slid the MicroSD Memory Card into the grooved slot of the reader and hooked it up to the D.C.S.'s computer. It rapidly uploaded and Dave located the file containing images from the phones camera. They slowly appeared a thumbnail at a time in date sequence: Photographs of the D.I's last year of life - clay pigeon shooting, on board a friends boat fishing, his grown up daughter, his baby grandson, pictures of another life away from his work. Pictures almost of another man...

The three men silently watched, all sharing in the sadness it brought. As the photographs materialised the date advanced, counting down, moving ever closer: a Christmas tree, birthday cakes, prize winning fish, smiling relations, a sunny beach, walks in the country, a toothless baby boy...and then the final two images: the first badly blurred - a dark shape, two glowing ellipses; the last image clearer - the final image Leighton witnessed - moments before death: A face certainly, but no human face, no recognisable animal either, though it had a primal stare. Dave clicked the thumbnail to enlarge it; slowly it filled the screen….. A face of pure hate and of fierce resolve; *the face of Evil.*

You old bugger…. Dave thought, *Leighton's only gone and given us our first hard visual evidence.* For all of D.I. Leighton's faults and misdemeanours, at that moment, Dave would have gladly shaken his hand.

Magenta

It was time, Dave thought, to pay the ubiquitous Sarah Nash a visit at *The Herald*'s H.Q. After flashing his warrant card at the front desk soon he found himself in the newsroom approaching Nash's workstation, an area of floor space demarcated with a Perspex screen. A cage may have proved more appropriate, Dave considered.

Nash sat typing in front of her computer, on seeing Dave she tilted back in her chair. "Well well..." she remarked, "So *you* are Dave Joseph? I recognise you from the university exhibition ... and to think...I thought you were just the hired muscle."

Clearly staff at the front desk had pre-warned her of his arrival. He flipped open his I.D. "*Detective Sergeant* Joseph," he corrected and then smiled, "but thanks for the muscle compliment."

Nash laughed, "It wasn't meant as one, but you can have it for free," She pulled at the tresses of her blonde, shoulder length, curled hair, "my my, policemen are getting younger!" Nash ogled him, giving a good mental undressing, her lips pursed. "You're the kind of policeman who makes a girl want to be really bad so she can get herself arrested ..."

"I'll see what I can to bring that last part to fruition." Dave replied.

"But I warn you Detective...I won't come quietly..." Nash let out a guffaw. "I'm glad you're here actually, I have so many questions for you. What really happened at that dig site? What is Kessler really like, apart from being a smartarse?

Dave ignored here, instead he was looking at her PC screen, "I see you haven't wasted any time?" The on screen article carried the headline *Corrupt cop in rooftop fall.*

Nash shrugged, "Don't you think it's in the public's interest to know when one of your lot turns bad - the proverbial rotten apple?"

"Corruption is a serious allegation, one which the force

deals with equally seriously. I hope you've got your facts straight Miss Nash?"

"Oh, I have impeccable sources Detective Joseph, and even when one such source…dries up…another readily appears in the wings…and of course we have a diligent legal department who ensure we avoid falling foul of the law." Nash smiled sweetly. "As you are here perhaps I could get a quote or two from you? You worked closely with D.I. Leighton; come on Detective, give our readers a real insight?"

As Nash's lips curled into a sneer Dave rested his palms on the sides of the desk leaning in towards her. "Certainly, I'll give you a quote. Just tell me, this story of yours…these *corruption* charges, why print them now, why not before…perhaps because Leighton was *useful* before? Feeding you tit-bits, the mangy cat that you are, in return for your not exposing him? Is that it? Did you suppress a story *in the public's interest* for your own gain Miss Nash? Were you in possession of information relating to criminal activity that you deliberately withheld from the police?" Dave pulled her keyboard towards him, "Let's see if we can make this article a bit punchier shall we?"

Nash, visibly flustered, uttered an ineffective objection as Dave deleted the word *corrupt* from the headline. His fingers tapped at the keys until the new word took its place.

BLACKMAILED cop in rooftop fall.

"Now tell me…isn't that a whole lot better? I used capitals to stress the key point…is that too much? You don't strike me as the subtle type." Dave faced her, "I'm onto you Miss Nash," seeing a pile of business cards on her desk he took one, "I've got your number."

As Dave left *The Herald*'s building, striding towards his car, a sense of deep unease hit him. He glared back at the building, cold 1970's concrete with a scattering of tinted windows staring back at him. It was a feeling akin to that he had felt at the dig site, before he had been floored, a claustrophobia, a closing in. It felt, Dave hated to admit, like a premonition. In his minds eye he saw the image Leighton had captured on his phone. Was this Finlay Stamp's *Soul Feaster*? Dave felt in his jacket pocket and retrieved the flyer on Almouth Monastery; he turned it to see Stamp's number. He pulled out his phone.

D.C.S Steele had, after some consideration, approved Dave's request to consult Stamp. Background checks on Finlay had come up clean, confirming all he had said as truth; he had worked closely with reputable and respected members of the clergy. With photographic evidence of the beast that had killed D.I. Leighton, Steele realised the potential value of a specialist, and right now the scruffy bed headed Stamp seemed the best source of advice.

The heavy feeling Dave had experienced in the car park of *The Herald* building had lifted the further he drove out of the city and into the countryside, a different energy tangibly relaxed him. On the passenger seat lay his document case, stuffed full of all he had collected on the various killings and the incidents associated with Kessler's paintings. Dave found himself thinking of the artist as he drove through the countryside, the open fields stretching out like patchworks in a quilt, scenery rich with vegetation, trees in full summer leaf, nature at its finest.

Somehow, amongst all the ugliness of this investigation, Dave's sensory appreciation had undergone a transformation. He noticed his surroundings more; he savoured the details. It was unsettling though, as he knew this was largely Kessler's doing, or perhaps more correctly something working through Kessler? It reminded Dave of a quote he had heard before but not remembered in full - something about taking time out to smell the flowers on any journey. The air that now pulled in through the windows and sunroof was certainly sweet with blossom, petals drifting on the breeze, field awash with yellow as far as the eye could see. With a long, slow breath

Dave took it all in.

As Dave approached his destination a melodious sound grew louder. In his rear view mirror he saw an orange and yellow ice cream van, complete with an oversized plastic cone above the windscreen. He smiled, remembering the lost pleasure such a sight and sound once gave. His parents maintained he could hear such a jingle three streets away; they teased him he had the hearing of a dog, and asked if he was going to start chasing the neighbourhood cats. But teasing aside he always got his ice cream: whipped white twirling to a point, drizzled in raspberry red sauce, a flake placed jauntily at an angle, completing the ensemble. The thought led him on to recall that as a child he swore that when he was older, with an income to spare, he would sample a new packet of sweets every day from the corner sweet shop, until he had tried each and every variety. The reality was the store had long since gone out of business and sweets swiftly lost their dominance in an older Dave's thoughts. Who was that boy, Dave mused, and to where did he disappear? He sighed, the ice cream vans tune still sounding in his ears, as his cars tyres came to a crunching halt on the neatly raked gravel drive.

Seemingly from every direction monks started to appear, some with considerable haste despite their advancing years, hoisting at their robes so as not to trip. The ice cream van pulled up along side Dave's car, tune cheerfully looping. Like excited children the monks shuffled into a queue outside the van's window.

As Dave exited the car he grabbed the document wallet. He turned to see a tall balding man with a goatee beard and wire rimmed spectacles emerge from the solid oak door entrance of the building at the end of the drive. The man raised his hands as he addressed the chattering line of monks.

"Gentlemen, Gentlemen, let me pass! Remember it is I who hold the funds!" The man smiled at Dave. "Detective

Joseph?"

Dave extended his hand, "Yes, pleased to meet you."

"I'm Abbot Michael; you're just in time for ice cream! Would you care for one?"

"Actually, yes! Thank you." Dave listened to the vans tune trying to identify it, the melody familiar, "Do you happen to know what that tune is?" he asked.

Abbot Michael stared over his spectacles, "I should say so! It's *Onward Christian Soldiers*! Do you want a *flake* Detective?"

Almouth monastery and its surrounding grounds struck Dave as a little piece of an almost lost England - charming and picturesque. The main building was built in grey stone, attached a small church with gothic arched, stained glass windows. The overall impression was one of stately elegance. A *retreat house* sat within the lovingly manicured gardens - a place where visitors could take refuge from the cut and thrust of the modern world and rediscover a simpler existence, the monks on hand to attend to practical needs and offering spiritual guidance.

Stamp had been noticeably visible by his absence in the great ice cream rush; Abbot Michael had however purchased him an ice lolly, with the explanation ,"Fin prefers a Zoom." The Abbot informed Dave that Stamp was tending the vegetable patch and the two men chatted as they made their way to the monastery allotment.

Dave took a chomp out of his flake, "It is truly beautiful here Abbot."

"Thank you,' Michael held one hand under his cone as it dripped vanilla, "We are extremely blessed to live here certainly."

A gurgling water feature bubbled water over slate, the remaining film of liquid left shimmering petrol shades of blue and violet under the strong summer sun.

"It is a joy to us that others come to share in our lives and our worship." The Abbot continued, "We offer sanctuary, and a little oasis of calm! I fear many have forgotten what it is to be at peace with the natural world. Our aim here is to provide a peaceful spot where an attitude of contemplativeness can work its restorative magic!" Michael's short beard was now considerably darker than his ice cream moustache.

"It certainly is relaxing here." Dave admired the dazzling cornucopia of rose blooms in yellow, salmon, whites, pale pink, and red, their scents combining and teasing through the garden air. "I'm only sorry I have to come all P.C. Plod like and disturb such peace."

Abbot Michael smiled, "We are pleased you came; no man should face what you are - alone. True, we live a simple life here, but there are certain things we have a deeper awareness and knowledge of, our strong faith prepares us greater in some areas than a modern mainstream education can. The brothers, Finlay and I have been praying for you Detective Joseph, we are glad you have found the courage to seek help from us. We know the internal struggles you must have faced." Michael's words were warm, his eyes understanding and compassionate.

"Tell me about Fin," Dave asked.

"His is an interesting story! We all believe he was sent to us - God's reward for our devotion." The Abbot smiled, "Though he was a... *challenging* child at times!"

Dave licked his ice cream. "Because of the Autism?"

"Yes. We suspected all was not well and fortunately he was diagnosed early." The Abbot paused, "The ancient part of his brain, the amygdala, functions differently. *Hyperexcitability* in this area is thought to be responsible for the social deficits typical in those with the disorder."

"And it made him a little terror?"

"More a little *scamp*.." Michael replied, "His surname is a derivation, our little joke, *Stamp* seemed appropriate."

"And Finlay?"

"Named after one of our dear, departed and revered brothers."

"Fin says he feels no fear?" Dave licked at more vanilla.

"Indeed. We thought him just a risk taker at first but he truly is incapable of that emotion."

"The perfect Demonologist."

"Certainly not a job for the faint hearted." Michael agreed, "Though of course in his case it is much more than a job. He was obsessed from an early age. Sometimes such an obsession allows education to be tailored accordingly, to engage an Autistic child. So we collected relevant literature and invited specialist clergy to compliment the stimulation we offered here. The brain is massively plastic you know? It physically changes accordingly to how we use it. Finlay has worked very hard to compensate for his condition."

"He is a credit to you." Dave responded, "How did he get his scars... he didn't elaborate when we spoke?"

Michael paused, "An early incident. An eight year old boy, also identified as Autistic, was orphaned in a house fire. His parents dead he was taken into care. A subsequent fire occurred at the children's home. He was dubbed a pyromaniac - a fire starter, but in his accounts he claimed a beast responsible. A priest became involved and Fin heard of the boy's plight. They *connected,* perhaps both sharing being Autistic. The boy responded to Fin. It became clear *dark forces* were involved. The boy Stephen was a target for the demonic, an innocent soul; a prized thing. Fin spent time at the children's home; he watched over Stephen, protected him as the attacks continued." The Abbot paused, muttering a silent prayer and met Dave's eye. "The boy was *taken...* despite Fin's best efforts. Fin put himself in the devils path - offering himself over the boy, but the beast tossed him aside, and in an act against God Almighty, claimed that poor young boy's soul right there in front of him..." The Abbots eyes filled with tears.

Dave smiled weakly, lost for words.

The Abbot sighed then returned Dave's smile. "I fear Fin's Zoom is going to be no more than a rainbow puddle if we do not make haste!" the lolly wrapper distinctly soggy in his hand.

Fin was energetically digging a patch of soil, throwing collected new potatoes into a plastic trug bucket. Shirtless and sweating heavily he wore sagging camouflage cargo shorts, which at hip level revealed the grey waistband of his *Next* boxers. The monks often became exasperated at this sartorial feature and it was not unusual for a brother to exclaim "Pull them up Fin..pull them up!" On his feet he wore some flip flops which on occasion lived up to their name flipping off as he drove in the spade with his heel.

"He works like a demon." Abbot Michael said, as they approached, "Oh forgive me Lord..." he raised his eyes, "A poor choice of words given the circumstances!" he threw Dave a cheeky grin. "Fin - lay" he called out "Your visitor is here."

Fin turned, raising the spade in salutation. He grabbed the grey trug and approached.

"Hello again." Dave said.

"Has the old man given you the tour?" Finlay smiled.

Quick as a flash the Abbot slapped the wrapped ice cold lolly against Stamps chest, making him flinch.

"Ha ha." Stamp retorted, taking the lolly and tearing the wrapper with his teeth, "Thanks, I could use cooling down."

"I will leave you gentlemen to it." Michael said, then turning to Dave, "If I may be of any further assistance please do not hesitate. Oh, and ensure you stop by at our shop and sample some honey."

"That's his way of asking for a donation!" Stamp winked, the Abbot giving him a sideways glance.

"I'd be pleased to and I'm only too happy to make a donation," Dave answered.

"He's all yours Detective Joseph, God help you." Abbot Michael turned and headed back to the house.

"Welcome to my world!" Fin said, in between long dog licks of his Zoom lolly.

"Now I'm here I can see the appeal." Dave remarked.

"Well, I could always use help with the digging. Here manual labour is seen as the antidote to idleness and idleness is considered the enemy of the soul, so don't stand still for too long or the Abbot will have you cleaning the gutters." Fin held the very end of the lolly stick; his hands coated in rich soil.

"A return to a simpler life? That definitely has its attractions, especially when I think of the mountain of paper work sat in my in tray." Dave was nibbling at the last remnants of his wafer cone.

Finlay gestured towards a white plastic table and set of matching chairs outside the nearby greenhouse. "I'm guessing you didn't come to join up as a monk?"

Dave laughed, "Not just yet." he placed his folder on the table and took a seat, his shirt sleeves already rolled up, he loosened his tie." There have been developments! As a result of which the Chief Super has sanctioned my consulting you. I have to reiterate the importance of confidentiality, but if you're still interested we would like your input." Dave unzipped the document case. "I have to warn you there are crime scene photos, they're not pretty."

Fin rubbed the soil from his hands, "One sec.." He handed Dave his lolly and grabbed the end of a coiled hosepipe nearby. On turning the squeaky brass tap alongside, frothing water spurted into his hands. Stamp washed the soil from his fingers and palms and when satisfied shut off the tap. He rubbed himself dry on his shorts and finally took back his dripping Zoom."Show me everything you've got."

"This is the latest and most significant piece of evidence, retrieved from D.I. Leighton's mobile phone, taken minutes before his death." Dave handed Fin a blow up of the image.

"*Soul Feaster*!" Fin exclaimed instantly, "When did this happen?"

"Round midnight last night."

"Figures...."

"We have managed to keep the *full* details from the Press. They assume he fell from a hotel roof. He was attacked

Page 116

before he went over the edge."

"Not many are fully prepared for such revelations." Fin responded. "It is just as well the press are in the dark, speaking of which…I'm guessing all attacks happened during the hours of darkness?"

"Yes," Dave confirmed, "and victims all have similar wounds - consistent with a clawed animal ..." Dave paused, "But then we both wear the scars bearing witness to that."

"Tell me. What was D.I. Leighton's involvement in all this?" Fin's tongue was now Day-Glo red with food colouring.

"My guvnor - strictly speaking he was heading up the Sinclair murder case," Dave paused, "It'll be all over the papers tomorrow, he was also the leak to Sarah Nash at the *Herald*."

"Hmm, the shit going to really hit the fan then? Oh, excuse me, is that an insensitive response? I should perhaps say I am sorry for your loss. Autism! Not always effective in such situations."

"Thankyou."

Fin studied the photo. "Dark forces, I have to tell you, are traditionally attracted to *the innocent, the ignorant and the fallen*. To understand that fully you have to think in terms of every thought we have as having ... its own ... *frequency*, like a musical note has a particular vibration?"

"Okay ..." Dave answered, anticipating his belief about to be stretched even further.

Fin continued, "Thought has substance, it's a transmission of sorts. Demonic forces have the capability to receive these transmissions. We are dealing with entities as old as time itself, with equally ancient knowledge. They can intercept these transmissions and determine through them who is corrupt. Those doing the Devils work, if you like, attract the greatest attention."

Dave nodded, "Certainly all the victims have some questions concerning morality - but who doesn't?"

Finlay's hand was outstretched, "Show me what else you

have?"

Dave handed the Sinclair crime scene photos over. Fin examined them, turning them from landscape to portrait and back again. "Fairly typical attack," he remarked. "And the cross? Too little, too late I'm afraid ... smashed through the window I see ... sulphur residue right?"

"Yes, that's typical?"

"A little piece of Hell left behind, *fire and brimstone*, a perverse fingerprint of sorts. The sulphur is what causes our scars to burn - we carry on us the *mark of the beast*, three scars mocking the Holy Trinity." Finlay's hand shot out again.

Dave poured the contents of the folder onto the table, enabling Fin to sift through and examine what caught his interest, he meanwhile admired his surroundings. The allotment was a tapestry of crisp lettuces, spidery carrot tops, full ruby tomatoes and juicy plump strawberries. From the building in the distance Dave spied an elderly monk moving towards them, a tray in his hands supporting a pitcher and glasses. Dave watched as he slowly, quietly, drew near. Dave smiled as the jug carrying monk arrived, nodded and spoke.

"Goodness ... what a hot day!" he exclaimed, "I thought you might like some of our homemade lemonade." The jug jangled heavy with ice cubes, and thick slices of lemon.

"Thanks Amos," Fin answered, "This is Brother Amos, Detective Joseph."

"Pleased to meet you, and thank you." Dave helped Amos place the tray on the table.

"My pleasure, can't have you over heating can we?" Amos smiled, his bright blue eyes twinkling just like a child's. "Enjoy gentlemen," he bowed, turned and slowly shuffled back in the direction from where he came.

"They spoil you, don't they?" Dave said pouring out two glasses.

"Ha ha." Fin answered, "What can I say ... I'm like a son to them all, even now they still fuss over me. I'm very lucky. Now that some of the brothers are getting older I can repay their generosity, take some of the strain off them - manage all the heavy stuff and - I've dragged them into the twenty first century in some areas."

"Oh?" Dave sipped at the cool lemonade.

"Yeh, we recently had solar panels installed and broadband, some of them even have Ipods and Kindles! We have a website - I designed it to market the retreat... there's technology, but it's all there in the background."

"All about balance I guess?" Dave said.

"Exactly." As he further examined the array of documents, Fin took a swig from his glass. "What's the score with this Kessler?"

Dave shrugged, "Where do I begin? I've met him...twice now; he is cooperative, very pleasant in fact..."

"I sense a *but*?" Fin interjected.

"He claims...inspiration comes to him from...another source he refers to as *The Originators*."

"Not sure I like the sound of that. Sounds like Necromancy to me." Fin replied.

"*Necromancy*?"

"Conjuring the forces of Hell in pursuit of Earthly power."

Dave shook his head, "I don't know what to make of it all." Dave admitted, "Somehow Kessler is connected, more than that...integral to all this. His paintings are more than just mere oil on canvas." Dave found the photo of Mantois painting. "You've read the report on this translation?"

"No." Stamp studied it, "Written in blood?"

"Yeh. Archaic Latin, translates to 'Their end will be ...'"

"*What their actions deserve.*" Fin interrupted, "Corinthians 11:15. Whoa, that's one hell of a calling card!"

"And at the Sinclair murder scene, Kessler's painting was molten, only to restore itself days later."

"Ah, that's just showing off." Fin remarked.

"Sorry?"

"It's telling. A Soul Feaster wouldn't be capable of manipulations like that. As I suspected a high order entity is what's really in control, working alongside the creature that kills. For such an entity disruption of the natural order of things, the ability to bypass laws of nature is child play. There is more to this than just a series of corrupt individuals being murdered."

Dave shook his head, "How can something be in possession of such power?"

Fin sat back, glass in hand. "It is said ... God first created Angels, the highest in status being Lucifer. But Lucifer was not content; he sought to *be* God, to rule heaven. Other angels shared his mutinous thoughts. God banished them and they fell to Earth with such force they created the pit to Hell. They swore eternal opposition. Lucifer was renamed Satan, he and his fallen angels retained their powers - immortality, mystical knowledge of the universe and the power to bypass the laws of nature - God vowed to protect man on the understanding man in return respected the powers of God."

Dave paused to contemplate, somewhat overwhelmed. Nothing in his life to date had provoked him to consider religion in this way. God, Satan, angels, demons, mystical powers, immortality? This all called for a major shift in his paradigms. He spoke, "These... forces? They are immortal?"

Fin looked up, "You can't kill something that has existed since the beginning of time."

Dave scratched at his neck, "So where does that leave us in combating these forces?"

"Our best protection is *positivity*." Fin answered, "Those at most risk of drawing the demonic undervalue life, lack any meaningful purpose. Dark forces thrive on transgression of the good."

"Prevention rather than cure?" Dave commented.

"Knowledge is power," Fin responded, "Man can choose to accept or reject Satan's influence, an awareness this choice exists is a start. Major breakdowns in religion have left man vulnerable to attack. There are droves spiritually adrift in our modernity." Finlay refilled his glass, ice cubes tumbling from the lip of the jug, a lemon slice breaking their fall. "Is there something you're not telling me?"

Dave's face betrayed a mild frown, Fin had noted it. "Why do you say that?" Dave's voice confirmed the suspicion.

"I get the sense, that there's more going on ... a personal investment somehow?" Fin's eyes made direct contact.

"You're right," Dave admitted "Though it's hard to explain...to do so I need to tell you about the ... reactions I've been having to Kessler's paintings ..." Dave pulled a sealed brown envelope from the pile of documents strewn across the table, ".and I want you to read this, it's a report into my parents death."

Naples Yellow

Abbot Michael studied Dave's face as the policeman popped the honey laden fragment of cracker into his mouth. "Now…tell me honestly what you think?"

"Oh…" Dave hummed, "that's good…" Dave felt a burst of creamy sweetness like caramel caressing his taste buds. "That's totally the business Abbot Michael, really good!"

Michael beamed, "I'm glad you approve. The bees are primarily Brother Matthew's domain; I cannot in faith take credit for the results of his endeavours."

Dave examined the jar from which he had just sampled. The label's design featured a simple black and white ink sketch of the monastery building set in its leafy grounds. Dave was instantly reminded of Kessler's wine labels; the artists imposing chateau with its twisting vines. Something about it resonated; it invoked a strange sense of déjà-vu, like a key for the lock of a room somewhere in the depths of Dave's mind had turned with a loud click.

"A penny for your thoughts?" Abbot Michael smiled. "Did we lose you for a moment? Detective Joseph?"

Dave snatched a breath before replying, "Sorry…sometimes even I don't know where my brain's at."

"Ah." the Abbot responded, "The perils of living in the modern world? Perhaps the mind craves silence; some relief from the constant barrage that affronts it?"

"You're not wrong there ... I'm changing. I used to feed off adrenalin ... My job gave me purpose - direction, kept me busy ... but now…?"

The Abbot nodded, "You will forgive me…throwing yourself into your work was once perhaps a distraction? I see many who come to take advantage of our retreat who once believed work provided an antidote to their pain. Quite often the bereaved for example…"

The words rang like a clarion call. Losing both parents early had shut Dave down to some extent. As a boy and a teen he had overcompensated, physically pushing himself, he would often run for miles, spend hours lifting weights in the gym, or attend martial arts classes chasing coloured belts. On joining the police he had worked every available hour, fast tracking his way to the C.I.D. And the rank he now held was all through sheer hard work and dogged determination. Kessler had reminded him his career did not define him - that life was also *emotional*. Kessler had penetrated his armour ... perhaps armour worn for far too long? These *changes* were liberating. "You are very right." Dave eventually answered the Abbot. "I am one of those people who, for a very long time, avoided dealing with bereavement. You are very insightful. You'd make a good copper."

Michael laughed, "I'm not sure about that! I am sorry for your loss though, and please excuse any intrusion." He smiled, "But know I am happy to listen should you wish to talk."

Dave was struck how rare such an offer was in the world he normally inhabited. Ironic when one considered instant global communication could now occur at the touch of a button. A genuine desire to listen, understand, and help a fellow human - such a basic thing and yet, almost a lost art. Dave stuttered his reply, "Erm...I'm not sure where I'd start."

"Who is it you have lost David?"

"I lost my parents when I was six. Theirs were traumatic deaths. "

"May I ask the circumstances?"

Dave took a deep breath as he collected his thoughts, "I was told my father suffered a breakdown...lost it ...killed Mum and then himself. He had been deeply depressed...disturbed ... aggressive...confused. His mental state pointed towards a verdict of murder then suicide."

"You were ... *told*? You have cause to think otherwise?"

"Very definitely and more so recently. Whilst investigating the cases I have been discussing with Fin lately I have become sure...there's some connection. And more than that...however afflicted...I can remember my dad, remember the *man* - he was gentle, good natured, loving in his way ... the whole case was whitewashed I'm convinced of it, and now I think I know why."

"Why?" The Abbot inquired.

"Because ... now I'm coming to realise there were *other* forces involved, *outside* forces...I've seen things with my own eyes that once I would never have believed ... I know there's an alternative truth out there. One many, would rather see hidden or denied."

Dave became aware he was having one of the most revelatory conversations of his life - in a small, quaint, sparsely stocked monastery gift shop. The man before him had granted him the space and freedom to shed his armour and speak openly. It felt powerfully emancipating, but even now Dave knew, if had not been for Kessler he would not be where he was, feeling as he did. Kessler held that key to the lock of the room inside Dave's mind. It was Kessler who chose to twist that key.

"I think..." the Abbot said, ".. you have unearthed some answers, or at the very least you are on the path towards discovering them." He paused then met Dave's eyes. *"Be self-controlled and alert; your enemy the Devil prowls around like a roaring lion looking for someone to devour."*

Dave's back chilled.

"Oh, oh." came Fin's voice, "If he's quoting the scriptures its time to leave." He was stood at the shop door, freshly showered, clothes changed and carrying his rucksack. Dave had agreed to give him a ride into town where he was meeting up with friends for the night.

"Thank you Abbot." Dave said reaching for his wallet. He handed a twenty over. "Keep the change... as a donation. "I have a feeling once my girlfriend Sam tastes this I'll be sent back for a truckload!" Dave picked up the honey jar.

Michael took the note. "Most kind, Thank you Detective, you are always welcome."

"No...Thank *you*." Dave replied. "For everything."

"I can see why the report dissatisfied you," Fin said, sat in the passenger seat re-reading the details of Dave's parents' deaths, "It doesn't come anywhere near explaining what really happened."

"I always had my doubts," Dave answered, "Dad was a fighter. He just wouldn't have done that...*caved in* like that. The breakdown he had...the moods...he fought them like crazy. I guess no child wants to believe a parent could do that...murder, suicide...but my instincts always told me it couldn't... *didn't* happen the way the report suggests, as you say it just doesn't add up."

"Didn't your Grandparents ever raise any doubts?" Fin asked.

"I think they were...I don't know ... *embarrassed* by the whole mental health aspect...they are of a generation that associated it with weakness... and anyway with no evidence of a third party involved what else could they do but accept the findings?" Dave shrugged. "I can't be harsh on them, they threw themselves into raising me, they would rather avoid the issue...to protect me, and I can understand how it must've been for them..... Hmm ..." Dave paused.

Fin looked up from his reading. "What is it?"

"Nothing really... It just seems that lately I'm better at the whole ... *empathy* thing."

"Ha." Fin laughed, "You should worry! Try being *Autistic*! Empathy's something I've had to *learn* - to try and become more *normal*! Mind you, if you ask me *normal* is hugely overrated! Another heightened response though, huh?" Fin looked back at his reading material "You put that down to Kessler's work too?"

"There've been definite changes," Dave answered. He pointed to the honey jar on the dashboard, "for instance my senses, they seem sharper...*attuned*...the taste of that almost blew my mind!"

"Ha." Fin answered, "I did tell you it was exceptional, I wasn't just drumming up business so we can afford a new green house."

"Seriously though..." Dave replied, "Lately all my senses seem to have been enhanced. I've noticed it at home; I have the T.V. on much quieter ... when I brush my teeth.... I feel the mint in toothpaste burn my gums... crazy little things in isolation."

"What about your father?" Fin asked.

"Huh?"

"Your father," Fin repeated, "during his ... *breakdown,* did he experience anything similar?"

Dave glanced at Stamp, "Why do you ask?"

Stamps gaze was enquiring. "Try and remember, do u recall anything? Did he ever mention it?"

Dave's gaze returned to the road. "Hmm... his *moods* ... they made him...*sensitive*...in a way I hadn't seen before. He was rock solid before ... a real man's man, so the changes were very noticeable. He began to weep at music that moved him; at night he would often sit in the back garden and stare up at the sky...for hours - this look of *wonder* on his face ..." Dave swallowed heavily, the memories pulling at him.

"So far ... " Fin said, "We have only really talked of the demonic attacking...killing...showing defiance to God, claiming souls that should rightfully belong to him ..." he paused, "What we haven't discussed...and I think may be really relevant... reading and hearing about your father, is...*possession.*"

The blast of a car horn sounded angrily, as Dave's foot slipped from the accelerator, the vehicle behind forced suddenly to brake.

"Possession?"

Fin pulled his rucksack from the back seat. "Cheers Dave. What you going to do now?"

"I'm going to see Kessler; his place is close by." Dave's mind was racing; he figured he may as well quiz the artist further in a bid to gain some answers.

"Be careful." Fin warned, now outside the open

passenger door, "Whatever Kessler's role is in all this he is in a very precarious situation ...subject to powerful forces."

"Thanks Fin and don't worry 'bout me, I just need to dig deeper. You have a good night."

Fin shut the door and saluted a wave as he hoisted his backpack on. Dave indicated to pull away as he shouted through the window. "I'll be in touch."

Lamp Black

Once more Dave found himself pressing the door entry button to Kessler's studio. An unfazed Kessler ushered him in. The artist was busy working on a new canvas. Dave spotted the detailed charcoal sketch that was taped to the easel; a fair haired woman, scantily dressed, perched on a river bank, in her hands some flowers. Dave felt the now familiar response, the rush of energy above his diaphragm spreading outwards...the nervous bubbling excitement, the double edged euphoria. The canvas bore some colour but little detail, coloured shapes like a view through heavy fog.

"I didn't think you worked from sketches?" Dave observed, recalling their previous encounter.

"Ah, true yes." Kessler replied, "It is rare, but in this case quite necessary...this is a strict brief; a poster for a ballet company's upcoming production. I have only so much freedom, the sketch once approved being translated to the canvas."

"What became of the last painting?" Dave's eyes searched the studio space.

"Sold! They sell before the paint can even dry." Kessler laughed, "Someone else now owns your nightmare." The artist's mouth retained its smile.

Dave nodded. He wondered what fate beheld the new owner. He knew it was a painting he could never have owned himself, deeply disturbing.

"I read in the paper..... your exploits with Professor Naismith at his dig." Kessler remarked, selecting a brush from the drilled wooden block. "Are you … recovered?"

"Yes." Dave answered. "Thank you."

Kessler dabbed at his palette. "Miss Nash had quite a field day. That woman, she has the ferocious energy and ambition of a Viking marauder!"

Dave laughed in agreement, his eyes drawn back to the sketch. The figure on the river bank had more than a vague look of Sarah Nash, now he thought of it, nothing specific, but it struck him hard at that moment.

"You have had a most eventful time of it?" Kessler added.

"You won't find me arguing with that." Dave admitted. "Hardly time to catch breath."

"Have you made any progress in your investigations?" The artist was adding depth to the dark waters that dominated the composition before him.

"We have been hampered by the death of Detective Inspector Leighton," Dave said, watching for the artist's response.

Kessler seemed unsurprised, "That.....is unfortunate; it has no doubt set you back?"

"He was savagely attacked and then fell from a hotel roof." Dave elaborated.

"Oh my. That *is* unfortunate." Kessler's tone was almost mocking, he looked up, "I am sorry to hear of it." he added, as if he had prompted himself to respond more appropriately. It reminded Dave of Fin Stamps wrestles with autism, "Forgive me. I live in my own world so much of the time."

"It'll be splashed across the morning papers…our department will have to face much worse, but I accept your apology." Dave smiled.

"And how is Sam?" Kessler enquired.

"She's fine." Dave replied, "Since the exhibition and winning your award she has had some interest from agents, a magazine wants to do a photo shoot. It has really boosted her confidence.

"I am pleased. It is a rare talent she has, a talent she must develop and exercise. I predict great things. Are you prepared for the changes that will come?" Kessler's voice was as dark and flowing as the waters he painted.

"Changes?" Dave asked.

"An artist's life is unconventional." Kessler replied, "Take it from one who knows! To create one needs much solitude. Relationships can be…soured…strained. In addition one can risk becoming somewhat of a performing monkey, painting on demand. One can easily find oneself...*prostituting ones talent.*" Kessler waved his loaded brush as a conductor might a baton.

"I guess we will take one step at a time." Dave answered, "Sam will always have my total support whatever happens."

"For that she is lucky," Kessler removed his glasses, rubbed at his eyes rapidly blinking.

"I am the lucky one, believe me......Are you ok?" Dave asked, as the artist clearly struggled to focus.

"Bah," Kessler exclaimed, "My dam eyes."

"Eyestrain?"

Kessler sighed, "Ah, that it were only so. I have a progressive disorder - *Macular Degeneration* ... I am losing my sight." There was a pause before he added "There are *worse* things than death."

For the first time Dave witnessed what appeared to be vulnerability in the man; facing blindness for any one must be an ordeal, but for an artist..? "Is there nothing that can be done?"

"Alas...No. The problem is one of blood and protein leakage and a subsequent destruction of the retinal nerves. Even modern laser treatment cannot seal the vessels. My days as an artist...are numbered." Kessler replaced his glasses and peered at the canvas, "Already what I see differs from others. I work.. as if through a hazy window. I see most clearly through my peripheral vision."

Dave watched as Kessler's eyes roamed the canvas as if he were reading a map.

"Work can be both a blessing and a curse," Kessler said, "It distracts me from the uncertainty that lies ahead but simultaneously places great strain on my existing sight; but for now I continue."

So Kessler was human after all - with all the associated frailties that brought. His riches and reputation could do nothing to halt the loss of his greatest asset. "I'm sorry..." Dave said, "I can't imagine what it must be like."

Kessler looked up at him, "Thank you." he paused, "This

is why encouraging new artists such as Sam is so vital to me. I have no natural heirs so therefore I nurture and support those who have the talent that soon I will lose." He held up his hands in acceptance. "All things must change. This is the way of the world. The cub soon grows and in turn challenges the leader for supremacy - we all must give way to the future bright, new things." Kessler laughed. "You have caught me in reflective mood Detective Joseph!"

In each meeting with Kessler Dave found himself charmed - in spite of the uncertainty of the nature of the artist's involvement with all that had occurred. "It's ok," Dave answered, "I spend most my time persuading people to open up and talk. This makes a welcome change, reflective is good."

"Ah," Kessler answered, "But these people they are suspects, no?"

Dave shrugged, "Yes - suspects, witnesses, or those in possession of some knowledge...withholding knowledge for some gain."

"Aha." Kessler turned to his painting, "and into which of those categories do I fall'? His black river now showed evidence of current, Kessler's brush flicking grey amongst the darkness.

"You tell me," Dave crossed his arms, leaning back against the work bench, "After all you're the one in a talkative mood."

The artist threw him a sidelong glance, "I'm sure I have no need to remind you Detective that suspecting someone of a crime is a very different...*fish* to that of proving involvement." He smiled a slow drawn out smile that showed just the tips of his canines.

Dave felt a shudder, like dripping jelly being funnelled down the back of his shirt collar. Kessler's dispositions were as varied as his pigments.

The artist attention returned to the canvas.

Dave took a deep breath, "We have growing evidence to suspect a *supernatural* force is responsible for the killings,"

Dave spurted it out, knowing if he hesitated he would question his own reasoning.

Kessler's brush stopped dead; his head turned. "Oh?"

"We have forensic and photographic evidence that supports this and both my own and a specialist's direct experience of encounters with such entities....." Dave was going for broke.

"You call Naismith a *specialist*?" Kessler almost sneered.

Dave raised his chin, "I'm not referring to Professor Naismith, "Why would you think that?"

Kessler's face betrayed nothing, "He was at the dig with you, it was in the paper, I assumed..."

Dave clenched his jaw, "Well thankfully in my field of work I rely on more than assumptions. Professor Naismith has been an ally to both of us. You would do well to remember that?"

Kessler inclined his head in capitulation.

"The specialist I speak of is a *demonologist*, and he is convinced the creature responsible for the murders is called a *Soul Feaster*. Does that mean anything to you?"

Kessler was mixing another shade of grey on his palette, lifting little blobs of white and pressing them into the previous darker shade. "My... you have been busy." he said, "Demonologists, Soul Feasters... I wonder how the tax payer feels at such *unorthodox* lines of enquiry."

Dave was having none of it, "I imagine they would shit themselves," he said, "But then it's lucky for them they're not the ones in the front line." Dave pulled his collar open revealing the scars on his neck.

Kessler squinted, saying nothing.

Remembering the artist's failing eyesight Dave moved closer. The artist eyes danced as he assimilated what he saw.

"What did it look like?" Kessler asked with excitement bordering on delight.

"*What*?" Dave answered, surprised at the response.

Kessler reached forward and touched the three raised scars.

"*Easy!*" Dave pulled back wincing.

"This *creature*, this...*Soul Feaster*; DESCRIBE IT!" Kessler's tone was impatient, demanding.

Dave stammered, "Uh... I barely saw it. I caught a glimpse... no more but..." Dave reached into his pocket. Before leaving the car he had folded the printout of the image captured on D. I. Leighton's phone. Kessler's hand snatched at the paper before Dave could unfold it. Kessler studied the image, light from the skylight helping his eyes focus, his head moving allowing his peripheral vision to scan. His index finger traced what he saw.

"This is it?" he said, not even looking in Dave's direction.

"Yes." Dave answered, "The last thing D. I. Leighton saw; he took the picture on his mobile."

"Bah!" Kessler dismissed the tragic circumstance, his attention fully absorbed on the image, "To *see* such a thing..."

Dave found Kessler's fascination ghoulish; the artist looked at the image of the beast with admiration and wonder, with no trace of horror at what carnage it had caused.

"I assure you," Dave said, "When I encountered it; it was no picnic!"

Kessler glanced up, "No, no, of course not....Forgive me... but for the *senses*, ah a feast yes indeed." He surveyed the image further, "A rare and monstrous beauty...."

"An inhuman, ruthless killer." Dave corrected, "Brutal and relentless and seemingly unstoppable."

"Then how is it," Kessler said slowly, "that you and your *demonologist* survive?" That mocking tone again.

The question left Dave open mouthed. Why indeed? In his case, the creature had had every opportunity to finish him off. Maybe Stamp's faith secured his life? "I don't know.." came his honest answer.

Kessler fixed him with a feline gaze, "Chance? Fate? Design? I wonder?" Kessler's eyes slowly scanned Dave from head to foot. It was unsettling; Kessler's clinical gaze was not that of one viewing a fellow human being, but rather one of a scientist examining a lesser species smeared on a slide under a microscope.

"I wasn't the creatures target obviously." Dave broke Kessler stare.

Kessler raised an eyebrow, "Perhaps that status may change in time?" Something of a smile played on his lips.

"Why on Earth would you say that?"

Kessler rinsed his brush, "You are all too willing to connect me to these crimes...am I in any shape or form connected to what happened at that dig? Hmm?"

He had a valid point."No." Dave admitted.

"Exactly!" Kessler held his brush aloft, "But you..." he smiled, "my *originators* who feed my inspiration, they talk to you also... perhaps you are as responsible as I, if indeed either of us can be truly considered so?" Kessler tapped at his bottom lip with the brush handle, "You see how...*interesting* this all is, what a tangle of threads there are to pick apart?"

"Mmm," Dave paused, "as usual you provide more questions than answers"

Kessler held his arms open, laughing uproariously, "I am only to pleased to assist!" his face retained a smile, "I urge you to think in more abstract terms. To understand you must look beyond..."

It was Dave's turn to laugh, his head tilting up to the skylight, the evening was closing in. "And *how* do I do that?"

"Meditate!" Kessler exclaimed, "that's a start.... but when you do...visualise not the stars...but the *space* between, the vast infinity that often goes unnoticed. Stare deeper and deeper; sink into the depths of space where a perfect nothing lies. Do not allow the brilliance of the stars to distract you; they are but players in a deeper drama, reliant on the dark to let them shine. Focus not on the surface Detective Joseph," he pointed at the canvas, "See the *whole* picture not just its component parts."

Dave looked at the painting, a work in progress at present; an impressionistic colour version of the sketch beside it. In his own mind he heard his voice repeating what he had said earlier when asked why the beast had not killed him. *I wasn't the creature's target*....Why *had* the creature focussed on those around him? - *Professor Naismith...the Night Hawkers at the dig site....D.I. Leighton...* Why was it *they* had become *of interest* - In some cases with fatal consequences? Most chillingly though, Dave recognised, Kessler was *correct*; these people had a stronger link to Dave than to the artist. Claiming Kessler was integral to all that had happened overlooked the stark fact that Dave himself could just as easily be some catalyst. It made Dave wonder who might be next to feel the creature's wrath. *God, please not Sam...*

Kessler spoke, gesturing to his painting, "Poor, tragic Ophelia. Driven to madness by love and grief. *One woe doth tread upon another's heel so fast they follow; your sisters drowned* - so it is that Queen Gertrude announces to Laertes, heralding Ophelia's watery demise..."

Heralding, the word sounded hollow in Dave's ears, almost as if it had been slowed on a recording device. *The Herald* ...his eyes noted once again how the figure of Ophelia reminded him of Sarah Nash...and earlier at the paper's car park...that *feeling*...he had it again...*dread*...*terror*...PROPHECY. The feeling was growing; it was overwhelming him with a fresh urgency. His heart was pounding hard; his consciousness seemed to be pulled toward and into the charcoal sketch: *Ophelia minutes from death*...A cold sweat broke from between his shoulder blades. Up above light faded through the skylight. Night had come.

Kessler was still speaking, Dave tuned back in to hear him say, "Ophelia when translated from the Greek means - *help*. Alas, when she needed it most...none came..."

Dave had his mobile to his ear, having speed dialled headquarters. Kessler turned to him on hearing Dave ask for Sarah Nash's home address.

"Detective Joseph?" the artist said, alarmed by Dave's obvious agitation.

Dave held up a hand, "Thank you…. yes I've got that…." He ended the call quickly, immediately selecting another number to dial - this time Fins. As he listened to the dialling tone he faced Kessler. "I'm sorry … I can't explain, I think Sarah Nash is in danger….I think she's the next victim….." Dave spoke into the mouth piece, "Hello Fin… it's Dave. Where are you?"

Blue Black

Lanyard Towers was a modern, seafront located apartment block with each apartment owning a balcony, where, on clear days one had unspoilt views of The Isle of Wight. Sarah Nash lived on the third floor of five.

She peered into her enormous American style fridge. The contents were sparse: a half a block of Cheddar, a tub of olive oil spread, a pack of processed ham - its corners red and curled - a pint of milk, and at the top, lying flat on a chrome rack, three bottles of white wine. She slid one free and pushed the fridge door shut with her hip. The kitchen gleamed spotless, a testament to its lack of use - cooking was something that went on behind the scenes in restaurants in Sarah's world, her expense account full of restaurant receipts stood party to this. Nash pulled the cork free, gripping the bottle between her legs with all the elegance of a docker, her short pink silk kimono bathrobe gaping open in the process. Having selected a large wine glass that could easily have doubled for a vase, she poured.

In her Art Deco style bathroom, water tumbled from the mixer tap into the claw-footed bath tub, the smell of Jasmine rising from the foaming bubbles. Armed with her giant glass and the now seriously depleted bottle, she bare-footed across the black and white tiled floor, placing her mobile on the Lloyd Loom laundry basket easy reaching distance from the bath. The wine bottle joined it and after a large glug of Californian white, so did the glass. She wriggled free of her clinging robe and tentatively tested the water with her toes. "Fuck, arse, balls!" she cursed, twisting the cold tap, sending a spluttering gush of water from the mixer outlet. Bent double she vigorously agitated the bath water with her hand until the temperature stabilised. Turning off the water she climbed in and settled her head back against the cool enamel.

With night closing in, Kessler became dependant on the chrome angle poised lamp beside his easel. Ophelia's feet seemed totally swallowed by the dark water that caressed her ankles; in the space between, tiny petals from her clutched posy floated tissue thin. Kessler flicked the tip of his brush creating brightly coloured coils - exquisitely bright fallen petals from her bouquet of daisies, pansies, forget-me-nots, violets, roses and poppies. To the side the overhanging willow tree, gnarled and twisted, threw a shadow across Ophelia's face, its heavy branches like Ophelia's feet seduced by the brook's dark embrace.

"Sorry to break into your evening," Dave said, as Fin jumped into the passenger seat beside him.

"S'okay," Fin answered, "What's up?"

"Well, either I've lost the fucking plot, or for some reason I've got this really strong feeling our Soul Feaster has got Sarah Nash on its menu."

Fin tossed his back pack on the rear seat, "What we waiting for then? Let's go"

Feeling the nice boozy glow inside, coupled with the warm lilting water around her body, Sarah Nash exhaled slowly. Steam spiralled upwards, swirling overhead; she placed her pale pink flannel over her face, her mouth sucking it inward, the cotton moulding to her features resembling some mummy from a B movie horror flick. Her peace was short lived with her mobile ringing from the lid of the laundry basket. "Shit." her hand shot out and patted its path to the phone pulling it under the flannel, "Yes?" she hissed. The voice that answered was abnormally deep, almost incomprehensible, Nash pulled away the dripping flannel, "Who is this?" The voice continued; was it a foreign language? Not one she recognised. Its tone rose and fell abruptly. It sounded disjointed - almost as if it were a recording being played backwards. "Very funny.....*whoever you are*....now go fuck yourself!" Nash ended the call with a jab of her finger. "Arggh!" the handset scorched at her palm; in a matter of seconds it had become searing hot. It leapt from her hand as she flinched, falling with a plop into the jasmine suds. "Oh fuck-ing great!" she fished around blindly eventually pulling it from the depths. She shook it, the screen stayed dead; she tossed it angrily against the far wall. "Oh fuck-ing great." she repeated, as she reached for more wine.

Kessler's eyes shifted from sketch to canvas; where once only colour and vagueness had been, forms took shape and details emerged. The slender bull rushes reached up from the foreground like teasing fingers trying to capture the breeze. The blossom tree heavy with flower jettisoned its blooms like confetti, a cruel paradox to the melancholy mood. Kessler worked at speed, strangely rejuvenated, his brush picking up colours, dispersing them, moving from one section to the next, the picture rapidly coming to life; weirdly beautiful in its tragedy.

"Jeez, I hope I'm not wrong about this..." Dave's heart was still racing, the sweat soaking the back of his shirt against the car seat.

"Only one way to find out." Fin smiled.

"Can you get through to her?" Dave asked, glancing at Fin, mobile to his ear.

"Nothing.... I'll keep trying."

Dave drummed the steering wheel. If being wrong concerned him; being right scared the shit out of him.

Nash's skin was starting to wrinkle; the once invigorating

Page 139

heat of the water was now distinctly tepid. She leaned forward, buttocks sliding with a squeak, toward the taps. She pulled the plug chain and heard the gurgle as water started to drain away. "Let's have a top up!" she cooed. She twisted the tap, alarmed to hear the pipe work vibrate with a hollow rattle. "What *now*?" she sighed, giving the mixer a smack with her palm. The pipes shuddered with a metallic thud. She twisted the taps off then back on again. "Come on!" Nash barked, and then she became aware of the drips escaping from the spout. They were not clear, not watery at all - but *red* and *viscid*. "What the fuck…" The chrome fitting started to visibly quake, the pressure inside dramatically increasing. Nash scooted herself backwards till her back hit the enamel. The drumming in the pipes became deafening, she clasped her ears, the noise growing louder still; the bath itself was now shaking, its claw feet dancing. The taps gave one final series of thuds and, with what sounded like a child's agonised screech, in a torrent *blood* exploded from them, showering the now screaming Sarah Nash.

The play of highlights across the sombre water's surface almost hinted at a face; perhaps beneath, in the gloomy depths, some creature beckoned? With head tilted and gaze downward, Ophelia's hair of tumbling gilded ringlets nestled on her slender shoulders; her flimsy gown barely disguising her form.

On impact the Soul Feaster shattered the bathroom window, propelling dagger like glass shards inwards, some glancing Nash's skin, her own blood mixing with that from the taps. Her voice was one long tearing scream as she huddled against the back of the bath holding her drawn up knees, rocking childlike. The creature flexed, achieving its full

Page 140

height, cloven feet crunching glass on tile; its amber stare burning, fixed on its prey. Nash's desperate cries rang out. Lanyard Towers with its select postcode had become her place of execution.

The voice crackled through Dave's digital TETRA system radio handset, from its dock on the dashboard.

"Sarge, thought you'd like to know we just got reports of a disturbance at Lanyard Towers, same address we gave you earlier for Sarah Nash."

"Thanks." Dave answered, "On my way there now. Better send back up and an ambulance. Will confirm status on arrival."

"Logging it now." came Controls response.

"Shit!" Dave punched at the steering wheel, "Don't say we're too late..." he turned to Fin, "Hold on." Dave squeezed his foot hard down on the accelerator, simultaneously flicking the switch to activate the flashing police strobe lights on the car's grill.

The beast tilted its head slowly from side to side, a steady sigh of breath lifting its rib cage under tight leathery skin. Nash whimpered, sobbing now; her body shaking. Tear filled eyes watched the creatures every move, fearful of its strike. Why did it hesitate? What was it waiting for?

Kessler stepped back, wiping the brush with a turps soaked rag. The paintings surface was sticky, wet with oil. For tonight he could paint no more.

The tyres screeched to a halt outside the apartment block.

Page 141

"Up there... look!" Fin shouted, gesturing towards the broken window three floors up.

"Shit, that's got to be it. C'mon." Dave flung open his door and leapt out, Fin not far behind, pulling his back pack from the rear seat.

"Take this," Fin said, tossing it to Dave, "meet you up there....I'll let you in."

"How...?" Dave's question went unfinished as he saw Fin take a flying jump and grab at the canopy roof shielding the main entrance. From there he hoisted himself up to one of the first floor balconies. Like a tree swinging monkey he continued onwards and upwards.

Dave ran his hand across the various door entry buttons.

"POLICE! Let me in." The door release clicked open, and Dave barged in heading straight for the stairwell.

Nash's trembling hand reached down between her raised knees; glass shards had crashed into the bath when the beast had smashed through the window. Her eyes were still locked on the Soul Feaster. If she was about to die, she thought, she was not going without a fight. Her hand slowly closed around the jagged object of her search, adrenaline masking the pain as it sliced into her palm. "Come on Arsehole," she screamed, "show me what you've got."

Dave bolted the stairs, two at a time, shirt wet against him, heart hammering, muscles tensed pumped full of blood.

Fin had reached the balcony closest to Nash's, a distance of about two metres. He climbed over the edge, hanging with arms at full stretch from the end rail. With a concerted effort he pushed himself away, turning his body one hundred eighty degrees mid air in the process. His hands reached out grasping the metal, fingers white. He hauled himself up panting. He had reached Nash's apartment; a warm evening, the french doors were partially open.

Dave reached the third floor, launching himself through the swing door from the stairwell. He sprinted down the corridor scanning the door numbers; he needn't have bothered, the onset of desperate screams was compass enough.

The beast struck - bullet fast, its unhallowed form little more than a blur. Claws tore at Nash's breasts, ragged tissue all that remained. Blood choked in her throat as she uttered her screams, gurgling bubbles of red, drooling from her mouth. With an echoing clatter the shard of glass fell from her hand.

Fin rushed to the door, hearing Dave's pounding, an accent to Nash's pained cries. He wrenched it open, Dave tumbling into the apartment, backpack in hand. Fin grabbed it as they hastened toward the bathroom door, the cacophony within sickening to the ear. Locked - Dave put his shoulder to it, metal from the bolt splintering the wood. He took a step back and kicked full force; timber tore and chewed into splinters. Another kick, the door flew open, slamming inward.   With momentum propelling him forward, on witnessing the sight that greeted him Dave pulled himself to a halt.

"Sweet Mother of God…"

Sarah Nash's body was hunched up at the end of the bath. Her eyes stared, mouth open, neck and torso laid open, the white of her ribs nesting amongst juicy red. She sat in a large pool of blood, the remains of the bubble bath creating pink foam on its surface. The creature squatted over her, leathery wings outstretched, its knobbly spine visible through stretched parchment skin. Its head spun round, teeth bared and bloody red, its eyes polished amber orbs dared Dave to move closer. Inside Dave's chest his heart felt double sized; he stood poised, frozen in time. The creature turned away from its kill, its cloven feet scraping against the lip of the tub, new prey now in its sights. With Nash beyond help, self preservation kicked in; Dave's eyes darted around the room noticing a free standing metal towel rail just within reach. He grabbed it, extending it out in front of him, the beast emitting a rasping hiss, the air sickeningly dank with sulphur, jasmine and blood.

From behind him Fin calmly spoke, "Hold your ground..." He was unzipping his back pack. "It's sounding us out."

Dave gripped the tubular steel, not daring to blink, beads of sweat from his brow stinging his eyes. The creature's feet shifted from one to the other, a bizarre parallel to the claw feet of the bath tub below.

"Be ready to hit the deck ..." Fin warned, "On my word..."

Dave, with eyes still fixed on the beast, swept his foot across the chequerboard floor clearing glass from his immediate path. The creatures head tilted, Dave could see the tension in its legs, coiled springs ready to release. It was just as D. I. Leighton had captured - evil embodied. Its hide covered ribs lifted, its pupils narrowed.

"NOW!" Fin shouted.

Dave threw himself down, simultaneously tossing the towel rail toward the beast, only to see it swatted aside, clattering and bouncing to the floor. The creature sprung from its perch in a scream of attack. It was headed for Fin. Dave anxiously craned his neck.

On its launch Fin had squeezed the base of the litre water bottle he held, liquid jetting from the pulled up nozzle. On contact the fluid fizzed and steamed, the beast's battle-cry transformed to an agonised shriek. Fin was chanting something Dave assumed to be Latin. Fin increased his grip, compacting the bottle, its contents cascading and stabbing at the beast, forcing it back. With one last throttled howl it smashed through what remained of the bathroom window, out and up into the night sky. In seconds its form had melted into darkness.Dave jumped up and peered after it, his forearms bleeding from contact with broken glass.

"Here." Fin tossed Dave a hand towel,

"Thanks." as he dabbed at his wounds he nodded to the

bottle in Fin's hand, "Don't tell me... *holy water* right?"

In the distance police and ambulance sirens wailed, drawing closer.

Fin smiled, "Well.... it's not Evian"

Ultramarine

It was well after midnight before Dave arrived home with Fin in tow. Sam leapt from the sofa hearing the key in the door. Dave had phoned earlier explaining as best he could the night's events and requesting Fin use their spare room in which to crash.

"Look at you," Sam said, noting Dave's arms covered in scratches, his shirt dirty and torn, "Are you ok?"

Dave shrugged, "Yeah it's nothing; looks worse than it is. I just look a mess, don't worry, I'm fine. This is Fin Stamp.."

Sam smiled warmly and extended her hand, "Hi."

"Pleased to meet you," Fin said, shaking her hand. "I'm sorry to bring your fella back in such a state"

"You brought him *back* that's the main thing…thank you. I can hardly believe what you've both been through. I'm just so grateful Dave wasn't alone. You both must be hungry? Up all night…giving statements…. Can I fix you something to eat or drink? I'm sure you could use it?"

Fin glanced at Dave.

"Don't look to him!" Sam joked, "He's *always* hungry. Bacon sarnies and tea do you?"

"Sounds great, if it's no trouble." Fin replied.

"None at all. Make yourself at home and I'll get those teas."

"Thanks Wombat." Dave squeezed her hand as she headed to the kitchen.

"*Wombat*?" Fin mouthed.

Dave laughed, "Pet name. Long story. Don't use it in company usually!" He looked down at his shirt, "Listen, I'm going to scrub up a bit, I'll be back when I smell cooked pig. You just chill." He called into the kitchen, "I'm going to get cleaned up love. See you in a few."

Fin spotted the easel set up near to where Sam was firing up the grill, the kitchen area de-marked by granite worktops in the open plan apartment. "Can I see what it is you're working on?" Fin gestured to the canvas.

"Go ahead," Sam said, peering into the grill, "Early stages though....strange story to it actually…I had this weird dream, trying to paint what I can remember."

Fin went to the easel, dropping his backpack by the sofa. "You dreamt of this place?"

"Yeah, pretty much." Sam arranged soldier rows of bacon on the grill plate.

The canvas showed what in Fin's eye appeared to be a fairytale castle, in lush fertile surroundings and a sketchy human figure with what must be a dog, both dwarfed by the imposing structure.

"It's Kessler's place in France," Sam called out, "I recognise it from his wine labels. Funny I should dream of it."

"And the man with the… umm it *is* a dog isn't it?" A bread roll came flying at him from the kitchen, catching the back of his head.

"Cheeky bugger! Course it's a bloomin dog!" Sam laughed.

Fin caught the bread projectile before it hit the floor, "Sorry," he grinned, "I'm guessing you just added that? It's not to...um... developed."

Sam joined him by the easel, "Hmm, I see what you mean, it could easily be a hairy pig... or a goat... oh dear, poor Fido."

"I guessed dog," Fin reminded her.

"Well you're right." She paused for thought, "I…remember dreaming of a man walking his dog. Trouble is, I can't remember what either looked like. Dreams are like that though aren't they? Impressionistic?" She examined the canvas. "Now I look at it I'm not sure he belongs there, he looks at odds…."

"Is it Kessler perhaps?" Fin asked.

Good lord no! This was an *old* man… *frail*…oh I don't know who he was, pure imagination. Maybe I just ate too much cheese!" Sam reclaimed the bread roll from Fin. "Ketchup? Brown sauce? How do you take your tea?"

"White, one sugar and brown sauce, but the latter on the bacon," came Fin's reply.

"I'm not *that* scatty," Sam laughed.

"She is!" Dave was at the door towelling his hair, "She could represent team GB in Olympic scattyness."

"Put it down to artistic temperament maybe?" Fin suggested.

"You're not supposed to agree with him! You'll get brown sauce in your tea at this rate!"

Fin's eyes were scanning the room; he noticed the *RockPool* canvas hanging above the wall mounted fire. "Wow! Is that one of yours too?"

"You like it? " Dave asked.

"Yeah I really do, it's amazing. Could I get a print?" Fin turned to Sam, "I'd love a copy for my room."

"Really? Yes of course. I'm in the process of getting some prints done, and thanks." Sam was stirring tea and preparing buns with spread and sauce.

"Sam won Kessler's award a few weeks back - she's just finished at Uni and now she's on her way to being a world famous artist, aren't you love?" Dave spoke proudly knowing Sam herself would refrain from any self cherishing.

"Uh, I don't know about that…though things are exciting right now. That pic does seem to have captured other people's attention." The grill spat and sizzled noisily, "You boys ready for this?"

"Sure" Dave patted his stomach," I could eat a horse"

"Well sorry, only pig on the menu at this hour. Sit yourselves down you're making the place look untidy!" Sam bedded the bacon in the buns and brought them through. "Where do you think that creature is now?" she asked.

"A good question." Fin replied taking a man sized bite of his roll. "Demonic entities have no place in our world; that's why sightings are rare. It takes an enormous amount of unusual energy to enable their access here. They're powerful and can corrupt natural laws, but not for long."

"Hmm." Sam answered, "So back where it belongs?"

Page 148

Fin took a drink of tea, "For now, yes."

"But for how long?" Dave added.

"Honestly...? I don't know," Fin replied, "there's something very unusual about the pattern of recent activity; it's very specific. A spate of focused attacks like this is very unusual."

"The big question is *why* then?" Sam observed.

Fin looked at Dave then back to Sam; he hesitated to answer.

"You think it could centre on *Dave*?" Sam asked anticipating his answer, "Is that what this is all about? Dave is its target? Did he tell you about his nightmares, the reaction to Kessler's paintings?"

"And don't forget your *own* dream;" Fin replied pointing to the easel, "I don't have all the answers. I think you're both being targeted, Kessler too, but even with the benefit of my experience and knowledge I'm not directed toward an obvious motive." He took another bite of his roll, "None of you is dead; that's encouraging."

Dave laughed, "Don't worry yourself love," he said to Sam, "You get used to him coming out with stuff like that!"

"For what it's worth," Fin responded, "with the recent roll call of deaths your survival is markedly significant. I can sense the positivity and inner strength in both of you. These are great weapons toward your protection."

"Kessler said something similar about my painting," Sam replied, "about positive energy. I suppose with my involvement in Reiki... I'm in tune with that?"

"Neither of us is religious Fin," Dave commented, "not in the strict sense."

Fin laughed, "I'm not here to recruit! You both have your own spirituality and are empathetic people.... you have a moral compass; specific beliefs on top of that are not so important." Fin licked sauce from his lips, "Don't repeat that to Abbot Michael though!" He looked at Sam, "I know a little about Reiki, it's about harnessing *universal energy*, right?"

"Yes channelling it to heal."

"So… my understanding is, you actively encourage positive energy toward you and in return reject the opposing negative energy? That makes you a hard nut for the demonic to crack."

"Hmm…" Dave interjected, "where does that leave me?"

"I think in your case your motivation in becoming a policeman shows a strong innate positivity - a desire to help and protect others." Fin paused, "I think what most likely lies at the heart of your being targeted is your parents' deaths. I think it's what… put you on the radar, so to speak."

"Fin has suggested my Dad may have been a victim of possession," Dave told Sam, "he doesn't buy into the whole murder suicide explanation either"

Sam looked ashen.

"Remember I told you how Dark Forces are attracted to *the innocent, the ignorant and the fallen?*" Fin reminded.

"Yeh?" Dave responded.

"Without climbing on some moral high horse it's easy to see how recent victims slip into the *fallen* category. If I'm right about an attempt at possession on your father ultimately it was prevented, aborted. Your parent's murder was most likely vengeance…for its failure. Remember, at that time you were just a child…*their* child…what could be more innocent than a grieving orphan? Even now you still represent the *innocent*. I think you symbolise unfinished business…*but* like Sam you are not easy prey. If perhaps you had followed the same path as DI Leighton - sold out and abandoned your moral code you might well be dead now. Over the years you've probably become one huge major irritation to the demonic monarchy." Fin drank more tea, "It would explain your bombardment in the form of dreams and the communication through the paintings…a supernatural *war of attrition* if you like? Dark Forces are trying to grind you down, chip away at your resolve till they find that tiny chink in your armour that will allow access to…and ultimately possession of…your soul." Fin pointed to his half consumed roll, "This is great by the way, thank you."

Sam smiled, "You're welcome," though her voice betrayed her concern.

"Forgive me," Fin responded, "I know it all sounds deeply disturbing but you must try not to worry. Anxiety is something Dark Forces thrive on; be aware of what signals you transmit. Negate these forces what they seek. Remain positive; live fulfilling lives and be mindful of your actions."

Dave threw Sam a smile, "Like Fin says we're tough nuts to crack, made of strong stuff." he struck a bodybuilding pose flexing his chest and lats, clasping his hands together.

Sam laughed, "You silly sod!" she turned to Fin, "Doesn't your work ever worry you?"

Fin shrugged, "To really appreciate the value of life perhaps one needs to have faced the risk of losing it? Witnessing what I have has given me a greater appreciation of what life has to offer. What a precious gift it is. Knowing there are real implications for transgressions of the good provides moral parameters; refusing myself to indulge in negative thought processes focuses my thoughts on the positive - and life is richer for it."

"Hmm." Sam replied, "The importance of a healthy attitude?"

"Yup," Fin answered, "Time spent perfecting that is time well spent."

"Maybe that's the true answer to solving many of our world's problems?" Sam added, "A common goal, rather than differing beliefs leading to conflict?"

"I agree - religion hasn't always steered man in the right direction however well intentioned." Fin looked at the RockPool painting, "To have painted that takes beauty of the soul... it is the true nature of our souls that matters, not what banners we ride under."

Sam looked embarrassed, "I will definitely get you a *full sized* print as a thank you, for all you've done for us. Despite the painful circumstances I'm glad you entered our lives."

"I'll drink to that!" Dave raised his mug.

Fin mirrored the gesture. "Take great courage from the fact you have, thus far, prevented Dark Forces from taking hold. These forces no longer have the element of surprise; you are now aware of their existence. Cultivate the positive energy within you, shield yourselves from their insidiousness."

"I wonder why my father was chosen." Dave looked thoughtful.

"We may never know," Fin answered, "The demonic are opportunists and they strike at the slightest hint of vulnerability. Your father was in a low place, they capitalised on this, but they failed to possess him. He thwarted their advances. Their attack would have been relentless. I have witnessed such violence, such rage *and* the fallout, but your father fought and fought hard. He must have shown great strength, great courage. He denied them incarnate form and the potential chaos such possession allows. Be proud of him, your mother too. Their sacrifice protected many others from pain and torment. Be proud as I am certain they would be proud of you; you have their courage, their same generosity of spirit."

Dave was quiet, his eyes glassy. The dark stain inside him faded with Fins words, the stigma surrounding his parents deaths had lived too long in his heart. He had always doubted the official explanation but he had been in a minority. Even his own grandparents had capitulated, preferring instead to draw a heavy veil over the whole sordid affair.

For the first time Dave felt he could love his parents the way he wanted to - free from shame and remorse. He smiled at his new friend, "Thank you Fin. That means a lot."

After what seemed an eternity of form filling, further explaining the previous night's events at Sarah Nash's apartment, Dave and Fin found themselves in a bewildered looking Steele's office.

Steele licked at his index finger as he navigated the stack of papers before him, eyes at times noticeably widening, controlled sighs escaping from his nostrils. He shook his head woefully, "I can honestly say…in all my years…" his sentence went unfinished, his attention drawn to yet another confounding detail in the report. He leaned back in his chair, his hands rubbing first at the corners of his eyes then at the nape of his neck. "Gentlemen, the C.I.D. has a wide remit when it comes to the crimes it investigates: rape, murder, serious assault, fraud. In my career I have encountered all these in kaleidoscopic variations. Usually, despite these…differences there is some…*structure*, some known procedure one may follow toward a positive resolution; gears click into place, cogs turn, the machine of policing advances forward…" he lifted the stack of documents, " but this…. seems to turn everything I know on its head. Frankly I am at a loss."

"Sir." Dave spoke, "If you'd told me two months ago I'd be filing reports like these I would never have believed you," he paused, "but current experience has forced me to rethink many things. Added to this we have hard physical evidence to back up our claims. The time for denial has passed; we must accept this new found knowledge and recognise a fresh enemy to those we endeavour to protect and serve."

Steele sucked in a long breath, "I am somehow reticent at present to mirror your sentiments in a press release."

"I understand that Sir."

Steele continued, "I can only imagine the widespread panic that would ensue."

"I can see little benefit in revealing what we know," Dave agreed, "we are only just coming to terms with it ourselves after all. Containment for now seems a cautious and appropriate strategy."

"Agreed," Steel answered, "let's do our utmost to prevent any department leaks, God knows we have suffered enough on that score already," his eyes flicked to Fin, "Everything must be on *a need to know* basis. I must be extremely mindful as to who has access to this information."

Dave, sensing D.C.S. Steele's suspicion, turned to Fin who acknowledged the remark but seemed unconcerned.

"Mr Stamp," Steele continued, "you can I'm sure appreciate my predicament. This is new territory," he paused, glancing at the typed report, "I do need to acknowledge your assistance... and indeed offer you my thanks. You showed remarkable bravery... both of you did, but you are after all an outsider. I must therefore satisfy myself as to your candour?"

"It's *Fin*, call me Fin," Stamp replied, "and have no fear; I agree on your course of action. The public is not ready to deal with the Medias inevitable sabotage of such information. It's ironic that knowledge of an enemy our forefathers had - and armed themselves against - would now cast society into chaos. I have seen many directly affected by what we speak of, lives destroyed or left in ruins and even amongst those there is often still a stark denial of the truth."

Steele nodded as he listened.

Dave saw in his superior what he himself had experienced on his first meeting with Stamp, that strange contradiction; a scruffy eloquence. "What will you tell the press Sir?"

D.C.S. Steele's brow furrowed, " With Nash being one of their own they will no doubt push hard for answers... for now I will continue in the same vein as I have with the previous attacks - we are gathering forensic evidence to assist us in the identification of a brutal killer. I will therefore reiterate that, unlike in the plethora of television crime dramas, collation of such material takes time. That should for the moment grant us respite; at least one may only hope for so much." Steele ran his thumb down the side of the sheaf of reports, as a child might activate a flicker book of crude animations, "It would seem I have some *research* to do of my own." He looked up, "Will you assist me in that… Fin?"

"I would be only too happy to do so." Fin replied, "Consider me at your disposal".

"I read that you drove this… *thing* away with *Holy water*?" the words escaped Steele's mouth with difficulty.

"Yes," Fin patted the backpack between his feet, "I always carry a couple of bottles. Never leave home without it!"

Steele raised an eyebrow.

Fin unzipped his bag and pulled out a plastic water bottle, "Charged with the *power of the positive*, think of it in those terms if you find it easier. We are fighting negative energy, simple physics really."

Steele nodded, "And… how does one *obtain* it?"

Fin zipped the bottle back in place, "You need a priest to bless it - I get mine to do me a job lot," he shrugged, "it's just a question of scaling it up to requirement."

"Hmm," Steele answered, "so do I arm my officers with it along side their pepper spray?" he shook his head, "Whatever next? Silver bullets? Stakes?"

"Silver bullets is werewolves Chief, stakes for vampires. I haven't encountered those…yet." he threw Dave a side glance.

Dave intervened, "It's a new enemy Sir, and quite clearly it requires some adaptation in combating it."

Another deep sigh escaped Steele's nose, "How do we overcome it?"

Fin shook his head, "We don't and we can't. We learn to live with it; we guard ourselves against drawing it to us in the first place. We cannot defeat an enemy older than time itself, one able to defy natural laws. We must live with the Beast. Its existence serves to remind us of the paths we should all follow and avoid. Our best defence is our own self control. As the pioneers of radar during the Second World War monitored our skies for invading forces, so these Dark Forces watch for our weaknesses, locking on to our transmissions. Once isolated and identified a source becomes a target, a dark inner hunger prevails, a demonic agent is dispatched, its bounty - *The Human Soul*. It is us who draws the Beast. We grant it its visa."

"Unfortunately…" Steele replied, "It is us the public look to for protection. Whilst man wakes up to his own responsibility, if indeed he ever can, it falls to us to deal with those caught in the crossfire. A thankless task I fear?"

"Just a tiny step to your left....that's it, perfect." The camera flash fired; soft, diffused light illuminated Sam as she stood beside her award winning painting. The photographer checked the image on the camera's viewing screen, "I think that will do me," he turned, "she's all yours Fiona."

"Thanks Ross." Fiona Stone, reporter with *Lifestyle* magazine, replied, gesturing toward the sofa area, "Perhaps we could do the interview here?"

Sam nodded, "Of course, whatever works best for you"

"Righty - Ho then Ladies. I'll leave you both to it," said the photographer as he packed his gear, "I'll email you the images this arvo Fiona. Thanks for the tea and biscuits Sam, been a pleasure snapping you!"

"You're welcome." Sam laughed. "Always good to get onside with a photographer. Make sure you choose a shot that flatters!"

"Not a problem in your case dear," Ross winked.

"You Charmer. I could get used to all this flattery," Sam replied, now seated on the sofa, Fiona in the chair opposite.

"I think you're going to need to....." Ross shook his head as he looked at the painting.

Sam blushed, "Thank you. As long as I can keep painting and people like what I do; I'll be happy"

Fiona scribbled in her note pad.

Sam's eyes darted to her, "Oh have we started?"

"It's a nice line, shows your humility. It's refreshing not to be dealing with pretentiousness!"

"Amen to that!" Ross added, "And on that note Ladies, I'm off to photograph an interior designer and his sausage dog. Wish me luck...I fear the worst! I know my way out, thanks again." He hoisted his bag on his shoulder.

As Ross left Fiona settled back in her chair. "This your first interview?"

"Yes." Sam admitted, "Does it show?"

"Don't worry; our magazine as you can tell from its title is rather light and fluffy. Our readers will be interested in you as an artist? What influences you, how you work, nothing too probing"

"Detective Chief Superintendent Steele, your statement leaves a lot of questions unanswered. You can understand our desire to dig deeper?"

Steele held his palms out as more camera flash bulbs burned his eyes. "Allowing this press conference to descend into chaos will achieve nothing. The simple truth is I am unable to satisfy all your demands presently; an investigation is underway, the results of which are as yet incomplete."

The assembled crowd of reporters jeered and grunted disapproval; more flashes fired intermittently.

"Can you at least confirm there is a connection in the recent spate of killings?"

"Use of words such as *spate* is exactly what I have been objecting to." Steele replied. "Inappropriate and overly dramatic turns of phrase are serving to make the reporting of these cases unnecessarily alarmist."

More shouts came from the crowd.

At the rear of the function room Dave stood with Fin, silent spectators to the circus. "Just as well there's no rotten veg to hand…" Fin remarked, "A right ugly mob if ever I saw one."

Dave folded his arms, "Yeah, Sarah Nash would have been in her element...poor cow…"

Fiona Stone glanced at her notes, "We have a quote from Adam Farrell, Kessler's agent, referring to you as Kessler's *protégé*, his *obvious heir*. How do you respond?"

"Really?" Sam answered. "That's news to me," she laughed, "Enormously flattering but difficult to respond to really…I just paint. Truth be told I'm in my own little world half the time. I don't think in those terms; there's no grand plan."

Fiona's pen scrawled Sam's answers in shorthand, "More humility, the readers will simply love you! But...if you dared to dream, where would you like to see all this take you?"

Sam shrugged, "To a little place in the country? Somewhere idyllic...somewhere to continue being able to paint, to call home.....not desperately original is it?" she laughed, "I guess that's where I picture myself when I daydream…"

"Are we dealing with a *serial killer* Detective Chief Superintendent?"

"Enough, enough!" Steele rose from his seat. "I have been more than patient with you. You have your statement; print it and let me get on with my job. No further questions."

Come on," Dave gestured to Fin, "We'd better slip away unnoticed. I'll give you a lift back to Almouth."

"These bloody things seem to be everywhere, must be a storm brewing." Flying ants were striking Dave's windscreen in tiny sporadic taps.

Fin gazed through the passenger window, "Sky's getting heavy for sure…"

In the short time the two men had known each other they had become very comfortable in each others company. Little wonder, after all they had been through together. Dave was a little sorry Fin was returning home. Dave didn't really *do* friends. He had *mates* - some of the old college crowd, a few work colleagues he might share a pint and a curry with but Sam was his only close friend. Fin's companionship had been a very welcome positive amongst the predominance of negative events.

"You'll come in? When we get there?" Fin asked. "Abbot Michael will be glad to see you again. Clobber you for another donation probably!" Fin laughed.

"Sure." Dave answered, "I'd like that, and anyway I've had instructions to stock up on honey."

The dashboard vibrated as Dave's mobile rang from its perch.

"Can you get that mate?" Dave peered at the caller display. "It's probably Sam letting me know how she got on with that interview."

Fin picked up the phone, "*Menswear!*" he said deepening his voice.

"Silly sod!" came Sam's reply through speakerphone, followed by a laugh.

."Your old man's driving," Fin said, "I've got you on speaker though so don't be tempted to whisper sweet nothings."

"You really are a silly arse Finlay Stamp!" said Sam, "...It's nothing urgent. The reporter just left, it was fun.... mostly. All very friendly question wise. They loved the picture..."

."Well done love" Dave shouted, "Hope they gonna send us a copy?"

"Yes soon as it's done.... strange thing though.."

"What?" Dave's head cocked to one side, his eyes remaining on the road.

"Kessler's agent described me as *Kessler's obvious heir*; apparently they're calling me his protégé!"

"Ha!" Dave shouted, "Typical...agent wants a piece of you already! They're no fools; you're the goose that lays the golden egg. They can see you're a potential gold mine!"

"Fancy calling Sam an *old goose*," Finn interjected, "I wouldn't stand for that Sam!"

"I never said old!" Dave interrupted.

"Hmm...Just a goose then?" came Sam's voice from the speaker, "Gee thanks! There's something else..." Sam's voice betrayed concern.

" Love....?" Dave knew that tone.

"Fiona, the reporter, she asked if I knew the winner of

last years Kessler award. I did… vaguely - Liz Freeman. She was in the year above me then of course. Fiona asked if I knew what happened to her... I didn't..." Sam paused again.

"Go on love, I'm listening," Dave threw an anxious look at Fin who was also intently listening.

"Fiona was thinking of running an article about her to compliment the one about me…did a little background research and was horrified to find out what had happened to her. She was a very different artist to me...graphic... more into design. Anyway she won the award and left Uni; Kessler and his agent Farrell took her on. Everything seemed perfect; everyone assumed her future was secured. She began work on sets for a ballet under Kessler's tutelage.... then things started to go horribly wrong... I had no idea....." The signal from Sam's phone weakened, her voice breaking up amongst loud crackles.

"Love, you're breaking up…what did you say? What happened?"

Fin looked at the screen, "Must be interference her end, good signal showing here."

"Love?"

The crackles subsided; Sam's voice returned, her words chilling. "...on opening night the stage hands found her backstage… she'd tried to *hang herself*… from the lighting gantry," Sam's voice broke, "They got her down in the nick of time but she had this…. major breakdown. She's back living with her parents now…apparently hasn't dared to pick up a brush since ....none of us knew....we just assumed she was living the life of Riley…." Sam began to cry.

"Ohh love…" Dave frowned as he listened, "I'm sorry.. that's awful… no wonder you're upset." He looked across at Fin.

"I'm guessing this was all covered up?" Fin asked.

"Seems that way," Sam answered, "How could things turn *so* bad *so* quickly?"

"*Kessler*…" Dave replied, through clenched teeth. He banged on the steering wheel, "Try not to feel guilty love;

you couldn't have known... if you had, you would have helped, you know that love."

"And you need to stay positive Sam, remember?" Fin added. "This Liz Freeman, she went into things blind ... like a lamb to the slaughter...it's how we chose to react in adverse circumstances that counts, remember that we choose our responses. Liz broke under pressure...hold true Sam. You draw much positive energy toward you; your paintings positively radiate with it. You're made of strong stuff." Fin laughed, "I'd say in fact you were actually a *tough old goose!*"

Cobalt Green

"*St. Michael and the Dragon by Raphael* - painted in 1505," Abbot Michael announced, directing Dave's attention to the painting hanging in the monastery's entrance hall. "A triumph of virtue over Evil!"

"St. Michael is the patron saint of exorcists." Fin added.

"Your namesake Abbot?" Dave smiled

"Ah that I had his resolute nature!" Michael kissed the silver cross that hung around his neck.

"You would get on well with a friend of mine ..." Dave observed, "Professor Naismith at the university, a font of all knowledge when it comes to things Art." Dave rebuked himself internally for not having contacted Naismith lately; the professor had been a helpful and supportive ally through difficult times.

"You must make him aware of our little refuge from the world!" the Abbot replied, "I would dearly like to make his acquaintance; he may enjoy our library, we have some beautiful illustrated texts."

Dave nodded, "I shall phone him. He's a good man. I should like to share with him what I have found here."

"We are always here for you," Michael said softly.

"Right." Dave clapped his hands. "I need a box of your honey, Sam's gonna start buzzing soon the amount she gets through; I'm afraid you're inspiring greed."

"Oh dear. Greed is technically a sin…in this case though perhaps we should show leniency? Finlay, would you be so kind as to help our visitor?" The Abbot extended his hand. Dave clasped it, "You are in our prayers David."

"Thank you Abbot," Dave shook his hand warmly. "Take care.

Dave ran a cloth across the windscreen of his car; tiny twitching winged bodies clung at the glass, "More flying ants, ugh - they're bloody everywhere."

Fin called from the cars rear, as he loaded the boot with a

box of honey jars, "Storms closing in. Look at the sky."

Dark clouds swirled ominous and low; the air had clamminess to it.

Dave pulled at his shirt, the fabric sticking in his armpits. "I'll be glad to get back home before that breaks."

Fin slammed the boot shut and moved to the driver's side, "Thank Sam for putting up with me."

"She loved having you around - we both have." Dave extended his hand. Fin took it and pulled Dave towards him into a bear hug. Dave found himself patting Fin's back before separating. "I'm not sure she'll forgive the goose comment though ..." Dave smiled.

Fin held up his hand, "*You* started with the whole goose thing, not me."

Dave swatted an ant from his neck, "Jesus, that one bit me - little fucker!"

Kessler watched the dark clouds roll overhead through the vast sky light. He tapped the end of the paint brush against his teeth, deep in thought. The canvas in front of him was a dizzy swirl of thick paint in reds, oranges and yellows, at its heart blackness - a Dark Heart to a fiery tornado.

"This door is getting worse Finlay," said Abbot Michael, pushing his shoulder firmly at the entrance to the greenhouse. It begrudgingly opened with a grate of metal against metal.

"It just needs some oil," Fin glanced at the sky, "I'll bike into the village, hardware store's bound to have some."

"Well hurry, you don't want to get caught in a downpour." The Abbot examined some seedlings in a plastic tray, "I don't suppose you'll listen if I say take a raincoat?"

"*Raincoat?*" Fin repeated, "Who on earth wears a *raincoat*?"

Michael shook his head, "Don't blame me if the heavens open."

"Not even you are that omnipotent!" Fin joked, "Anyway I'll be as quick as a flash. Time me."

Kessler worked quickly. Peering through his tortoise rimmed glasses his eyes stared wildly, barely blinking. Ribbons of painted flames exploded from their dark core, his brush cutting centrifugal channels - untamed energy released from its source.

Dave switched on the wipers; more flying ants splattered the screen, "Where the hell are they all *coming* from?"

Fin tucked the small rectangular can of oil into the pocket of his cargo shorts and grabbed his mountain bike from where it stood, leaning outside the village hardware store. The gun-metal sky darkened further.

Almouth's greenhouse had certainly seen better days, added to the rusty hinges it had a few missing panes of glass, others remaining were badly cracked, battle scars mainly inflicted by the elements but also from clumsy monks. Inside Abbot Michael continued his repotting, carefully handling the tender young plants, humming to himself contentedly. Flying ants were catapulting themselves against the exterior glass, some had gained entry; their number seemed to be growing.

The sky was now dominated by lead grey clouds, turning and bellowing. Fin was stood up in the saddle, his feet pedalling furiously. He was off road now, cutting his way through country paths, dirt kicking up with his progress. He felt his shirt sticky on his back, ropy sweat on his skin. It was as if that day night had come early.

The Abbot smoothed the peeling adhesive tape flat, crudely securing the small sheet of clear plastic serving as a makeshift window repair. Some ants had been using it as an entry point. They flitted overhead, as more of their number sought alternative access, locating weak spots in the structure, quickly capitalising, streaming through the cracks in the glass and poor seals in the frame.

The Abbot returned to his task, teasing soil from the plant's spidery roots. A flying ant collided into the right lens of his spectacles, another bit at the back of his neck. The sharp shot of pain made Michael flinch. His glasses fell from his hand as he tried to remove the winged corpse from the lens; they clattered to the floor bouncing off the low shelf. Ants swarmed towards his eyes.

Kessler wrenched off his glasses and blinked rapidly. The dark centre of the painting before him stared back like a bottomless pit; a window to eternity, framing it a commotion of colour, chaotic, unfettered, the paint laying thick, glistening tongues of fire. The artist blinked again, knowing it would change nothing, his vision robbed of registering any detail.

The heavy tread of Fin's bike tyres cut deep furrows in the dry soil. His leg muscles worked hard driving the pedals faster, his forearms slimy with sweat, hands formed into tight fists around the rubber gripped handlebars. A heavy sky and the lush dense trees starved the woods of light. Fin found himself squinting to see.

Page 166

A seething collar of ants clung to the back of Michael's neck. He threw his hands backwards flicking at the mass of scurrying bodies, their tiny jaws like hooked anchors, their bites nipping and sour. His face had become an ever growing mask of bulbous bodies and scraping wings. A crunch underfoot; Michael's sandaled foot crumpled his spectacles; with eyes tight shut, he stumbled forwards.

Sweat pooled heavier across the surface of Fin's body, exuding from his pores, collecting as globules. From the dark inked form of his tattooed cross a different distillation secreted, red, thick, ruby gems trapped in the sparse blonde hairs. Fins crucifix was bleeding.

Michael's hand clutched for the shelf; his body lurched forward. His weight took the shelf with him, both tumbling to the floor. More ants swooped downwards, target in their sights. The Abbot rolled himself across the greenhouse's stone floor, trying in vain to be free of his attackers, his hands scratched at his infested features, now a writhing mass of ants five or six deep.

Blood poured in rivulets down the length of Fin's forearm, staining into his t-shirt. His head felt light; his eyes pulled focus. Still his feet pedalled; his teeth clenched together. Drawing on reserves of energy he kept moving, navigating the winding path, steering himself through irregular terrain. He knew he must get home and he knew he must do it quickly.

Kessler lit up a Menthol *More*; the long thin cylinder glowing orange at its tip. He agitated the brush in its jar of turps watching the paint cloud contaminate its environment. He squeezed the bristles between thumb and forefinger, milking them of their fluid, first a stream, then droplets, one final squeeze.

The Abbot had turned himself onto his front, pulling himself up onto all fours; his hands reached out in all directions searching. Ants were crawling up his sleeves, down his neckline, their bites relentless. With his left hand he felt plastic, he pulled at the container, his fingers feeling at its shape, he found a nozzle - pest spray - protection for the roses. He pulled it to his face, his palm depressing the plastic handle; he felt the spray's contents mist from the nozzle. Again he sprayed ... Again ... Again.

Fin jumped from his bike even before it had stopped moving. He crashed his way through the wooden gate leading to the monastery allotment and sprinted to the greenhouse. Even from a distance he could see the dark swarming insects inside.

Abbot Michael's ears registered the smash of glass, his hand still weakly pumping at the plastic container directed towards his face. He heard Fin's voice calling his name, hands brushing at his face and neck. He tried to speak out but no sound emerged and then he felt water; a strong jet of water.

Fin aimed the hose jet at the Abbot's face. He had needed to smash his way into the greenhouse, the door having inexplicably welded shut. Soaked ants shot from Michael's features, the flow of water forcing them in all directions Fin oscillated the hose head, keeping it moving. With his other hand he dragged the Abbot out through the breached door. Once outside he grabbed Michael's hooded robe pulling it up his body and over the Abbots head, still hosing him down, soaking the man, drenching him in his underwear.

Michael's eyes flickered open, his face red with weals,

puffy, swollen. He attempted a weak smile, his right hand rising slowly, markedly trembling.

Fin smiled back, "It's ok, don't try to speak…you're ok now."

Michael lowered his head; his eyes glanced down, seeing himself lying helpless, face up on the grass, soaked to the skin in just a pair of Y fronts. His brow knitted to a frown.

Fin saw the Abbots reaction as he shut off the hose. "Don't worry Abbot ... think of it as another baptism?"

Purple Madder

"Come on Daisy, don't give up on me now…" Sam lovingly stroked the dashboard of her VW Beetle. The engine settled again after a few splutters. "There you go baby, that's it girl."

Daisy was powder blue with a large painted daisy on her bonnet; Dave refused to ride in her.

Sam was unsure what reception lay ahead. She had contacted the parents of Liz Freeman, last year's recipient of Kessler's prize, having heard about her tragic year. Liz's parents had agreed to a meeting, but had warned Sam their daughter was still in very delicate health. Sam's interest was not wholly selfless, she was in the same position Liz was a year ago; she wanted to learn more.

Mrs Freeman answered the door, a homely looking woman in her fifties; her eyes were kind, her smile inviting.

"Thank you for allowing me to visit," Sam said offering her hand, "I'll try not to intrude for too long."

The two shook hands. "Liz doesn't have too many visitors these days…I'm afraid friends quickly fell away." The woman's voice was quiet, with more than a tinge of sadness.

"I had no idea until a few days ago what had happened." Sam answered, "I'm really am terribly sorry."

"Were you ... friends? Lizzy and you? At university?"

"Not really. I was in the year below. I admired her work."

"Well…" Mrs Freeman's eyes looked away "All that has ended now."

Sam paused, "It must have been a very difficult time…for all of you. I hope you can all find some way forward towards happiness again."

"Thank you." Mrs Freeman met Sam's eyes, the words received with a warm smile. She gestured to the stairs "Lizzy's in her room, to the left, first door. She is quite good today; she ate some lunch, had a nap. I'll fetch some tea up to you shortly. Go on up."

Sam thanked her host and padded up the stairs, finding the door to Liz's bedroom. She sighed, taking a moment, grounding and protecting herself, aware Dark Forces could be present, preparing herself as best she could. She knocked lightly on the door

"Come on in Sam," the response was surprisingly cheery.

Sam opened the door slowly and peered inside. Liz sat cross legged on her single bed. Sam barely recognised her. She was stick thin, her clothes hanging off her; a shapeless grey cardigan and white t-shirt, some faded black leggings tucked into stripy socks. Last time Sam had seen her she had had bright orange backcombed hair, now it was mousey and scraped back into an elastic band accentuating her gaunt features. With her high cheekbones it was like addressing a skull.

"Hello Liz..." Sam wondered why she found herself creeping into the room, "Thanks for seeing me."

Liz pointed to the foot of the bed, "Sit down. Mum's getting tea right?"

"Thank you. Yes." Sam sat down.

"No need to walk on eggshells on my account," Liz smiled. She picked up a tin beside and pulled out some cigarette papers. "Smoke?"

"Not for me thanks," Sam replied.

Liz had never smoked at Uni.

"I'm doing loads better," Liz stated, licking at the gummed edge of her roll up. "You're shocked though, right, bout how I look? It's ok, I know I look at deaths door, but I'm heaps better."

Sam smiled sympathetically, "You've been to hell and back Liz, I'm sorry, and I don't expect you to be beating your chest and dressed for the catwalk."

"Hell and back ..." Liz repeated, "Ain't that the truth." She smiled, tugging at her cardigan, "Don't you know this will be all the rage in Paris next season." She laughed "I've got some work to do, recovery wise ...but I'm headed in the right direction."

"Glad to hear it. One day at a time right?" Sam folded one leg under her, settling onto the bed. "What happened

Liz? Can you talk about it?"

Liz took a long draw from her roll up, snapping the Zippo lighter shut in her hand. Sweet musky tobacco scent filled the air.

Sam noticed Liz's chewed nicotine stained fingernails.

"The official line is I've got an extreme form of *Obsessive Compulsive Disorder*. I'm on meds for it now. I certainly feel the difference. Tired a lot ... but at least I sleep soundly now ... no more bad dreams. She tapped her head. "Touch wood."

"You were having regular nightmares?"

Liz visibly shuddered, "Was I ever..." she took another draw. "Vivid painful nightmares, truly horrific...of death, torture...murder; and during the day I'd get unwanted thoughts, overwhelming urges... the thoughts growing more and more intrusive. Urges to harm others.... self sabotaging thoughts," Liz met Sam's eyes, "you know what I did don't you? How it all came to a head?"

Sam nodded, "Yes I do," she paused, "I can't imagine how it was for you, but as you say yourself you're feeling better now... towards recovery."

"Yeah," Liz agreed, "I've got help now, good help. I see a cognitive behaviour therapist, she's great and my folks... they've been brilliant throughout."

"You're sure you're ok talking about this...not too raw?" Sam tilted her head to one side.

"I like you," Liz answered, "you're sensitive but direct. I wish we'd hung out more at Uni."

"Different years..." Sam replied, "You had masses of friends anyway."

Liz looked at the smoke ring she had formed, "Yeah...Where are they now?" The smoke ring dispersed, she traced a circle where it had been... "All gone..."

"Fair weather friends?" Sam smiled, "I was once told people come into our lives for a reason, a season or a lifetime. Perhaps they were the seasonal variety?"

"You make them sound like vegetables," " Liz laughed, "and not far wrong in some cases!"

Sam laughed too, glad to have lightened the mood.

"Of course trying to hang myself from a ballet stage didn't help when it came to keeping or making friends." Liz stubbed out her roll up in a nearby saucer, "That had the few remaining ones running for the hills."

Sam hesitated then spoke, "What drove you that far?"

Liz folded her arms, tucking her hands into the opposing sleeves of her enormous cardigan, "You know I told you about the thoughts, the crazy ideas?"

Sam nodded.

"Well, let me tell you the kind of thoughts that led up to what I did." Liz closed her eyes momentarily, took a breath and then continued, "One time I was in the Underground and I had this overwhelming urge to push this old woman in front of the incoming train. I got close behind her, realised she would need quite a shove...the train was getting closer, I braced myself...all geared up to push and at the last minute she walked away down the platform. If she hadn't, I'm sure I would have pushed her."

"That's dreadful Liz; you felt that out of control?"

"Another time I was on an escalator, in front of me there was a mother carrying a toddler, I got this wild idea to snatch the child... toss it over the side."

Sam gasped, unable to hide her horror.

"I know..." said Liz, "that was what was happening. Thoughts of suicide too, I guess I explored every method there is, at one time or another."

"When did this all start?" Sam asked, "You weren't like this at Uni?"

"Started with Kessler."

Sam felt a chill ripple through her.

"The shrink said it was down to stress induced pressure, suddenly being thrust into the Art world and all that went with it."

Sam's expression was questioning.

"Coke." said Liz, "I tried it, though not for long, but shrink said it probably contributed. It was stupid I know."

"Kessler got you on coke?"

"No, I give him that due, he was dead against drugs. It was the others in the art fraternity. Kessler was always kind but...." Liz's voice trailed off.

"But what?"

"Kessler was never unkind; he gave me opportunities I could never have had otherwise. It was just...."

Sam hung on her words.

".....I felt like I was being *groomed*."

A knock came at the door followed by the appearance of Mrs Freeman carrying a tray holding two mugs and a plate of biscuits.

Liz yawned.

"You're tired Lizzy." Mrs. Freeman placed the tray between her daughter and Sam, "I think maybe that's enough excitement for today?" she turned to Sam, "I'm sure Sam understands?"

"Of course." Sam answered.

Liz took a biscuit. She nibbled one edge then replaced it on the plate, "I do feel tired," she looked at Sam, "it comes in waves."

Sam picked up a mug and stood, "Don't worry. I'll chat with your Mum while I finish my tea, you rest."

She smiled at Mrs Freeman, who ushered her to the door. "I'll see you again Liz."

Liz had curled up on the bed in a foetal position, her breathing already heavier.

As Sam left she pondered, *groomed* for what?'

"Ok mate...well give him my best and let me know if there's anything I can do? Ok...cheers then, bye." Dave pressed end call on his mobile, "Jesus!"

"What is it?" Sam asked from the sofa.

"It's Abbot Michael; he got attacked by a swarm of those pesky flying ants...they bit him to buggery. Poor bloke's in hospital swollen up like a barrage balloon."

"Oh no. Is he going to be alright?" Sam stood up.

"Yeah, I think they were worried in case he was allergic; they've pumped him with steroids to combat the swelling...he'll be fine. One of those bastards bit me up at the Monastery, evil little fuckers."

"They don't usually bite...or attack in a swarm?" Sam remarked, "What's going on?" her eyes became teary, "This is all part of it...isn't it...is anyone safe? Are *we* safe?" Sam shook her head, "Where is this all going to end?"

Dave bit at his top lip, "God alone knows love," he took her hands, "Come here..." he hugged her tight, "I know it's hard love, it seems like one thing after another. But like Fin said, we have to make sure we don't buckle. We'll be alright...we'll be safe because we *choose* to refuse entry to these...*forces*. They may have taken knocks at us and hurt those around us but we're ok aren't we...and we are still fighting right? They'll probably try every trick in the book but we're not scared of a fight are we...? Hmmm?"

Sam placed her head on Dave's chest. He kissed her forehead and held her tight. His eyes looked above the fireplace at Sam's beautiful painting, the water in it looked so still, so cool.

Dioxazine Purple

"I promise I'll be careful, don't worry…anyway what can possibly happen in a public place during the day?" Sam had contacted Kessler and asked to meet with him. Dave wasn't overjoyed at the prospect with all that had transpired but he could fully understand Sam's desire for an explanation regarding Liz Freeman.

The artist had suggested he and Sam meet in Victoria Park, by the *Chinese Bell* - a memorial featuring a Chinese bell in a miniature pagoda, which was erected by the crew of *HMS Orlando* in honour of their fallen shipmates, killed during the campaign to relieve Peking in 1900.

Sam parked up *Daisy* and made her way through the park; it was another bright day and the flower beds were bursting with blooms; ground staff were busy cutting the turfed areas and neatly trimming the edges of the beds with regimental efficiency. The park was being enjoyed by a scattering of people: mothers with buggies containing floppy hatted infants shielded from the strong rays of the sun, student types lounged - some reading paperbacks, others sunbathing with iPods plugged in; their toes twitching to rhythms they furtively enjoyed. The ice cream van was doing a roaring thanks to the kiddies' playground and every so often a business type walked by with a jacket casually slung over one shoulder, enjoying a temporary hiatus from their corporate prison. Sam passed the large fountain nearing the pagoda and spied Kessler walking toward her on the opposite path. He was dressed she thought more for Cannes than Portsmouth City Centre, in white linen trousers and grey sandals with a pale grey polo shirt and some very expensive looking Ray- Ban Clubmaster sunglasses. She wondered if he ever looked underdressed.

Kessler raised a hand, his manner relaxed and friendly. "Good Morning…is it still morning?"

Sam glanced at her watch, "Just! It's a little before noon."

"I rarely wear a watch," Kessler replied, "and, as I am

sure David told you, I struggle to see anything bigger than a bus these days."

The two of them were now at the memorial. Sam had been nervous, but on hearing the artist remind her of his failing eyesight her empathetic side kicked in, "Yes..I am sorry to hear of it. How is your sight?"

"It is a good excuse to wear expensive eyewear!" Kessler said disarmingly. "I can see *you* perfectly well though, and may I say you are looking a most exquisite vision dressed in your Batik."

"Oh..thankyou." Sam replied, "It's a traditional Javanese pattern - indigo, dark brown, and white supposedly representing the three major Hindu Gods. I brought it online! Unfortunately haven't been to that part of the world as yet!"

"Well put it on your list," Kessler responded, "travel provides much inspiration, and it is one bonus of commercial success."

Sam smiled, "It is a dream to travel more, Dave and I had to save and put most of what we have into the house. Even visiting my parents has proved difficult."

"Where do they reside?"

"They're in France; they live about a thirty minute drive from Aix en Provence in a village called Villemus."

"I know it. A very pretty place. I should have guessed with a surname of Paris there was a French connection!"

Sam laughed, "Well you would think so, but they are fairly new residents; they sold up and moved there when Dad retired. They have a lovely place...very rustic, stone built. Dad's always tinkering away and doing D.I.Y. Drives Mum wild!"

Kessler laughed. "Well I am very happy in my abode across the Channel; I am lucky I have great staff around me who feel more like family than mere employees. Family is one thing I do not have so I urge you to cherish yours."

"We are saving to spend Christmas with them. So it won't be long, I miss them of course. Dave could use a holiday too..."

"It has been a difficult time for him."

Sam realized Kessler had totally charmed her. Her reservations about him, the questions about Liz Freeman that had burned within for days, had dissolved in his company. He seemed totally without threat.

Sam paused before answering. "That's putting it mildly. He rarely has a nights sleep without disturbance these days. He has had to cope with so much lately..."

"He told me of his nightmares...what do you make of it all Sam? What are your impressions?" Kessler gestured to the park bench close by and the two of them sat down.

"To say we have been on a rollercoaster sounds clichéd...but it's certainly felt like a white knuckle ride...and seemingly one with no end to it. The two of us have had to pretty much rethink everything belief wise...now we accept things that previously we would have considered fantastical. It's a strange place we find ourselves in. Sometimes I wish we could just go back to how things were before...but there is no going back. And there are so few with whom we can share what we have learned, only those who have had direct experience. People like you..."

Kessler nodded, listening intently. "What do you consider *my* experience is?"

"The jury's out on that one to be honest."

"Would you believe me if I tell you I would never deliberately hurt either you or David?"

"I hope that is true; I have seen nothing personally in you to make me think otherwise. Your part in all that has happened though seems very uncertain. Your inspiration seems to share something with Dave's nightmare imaginings... part of me wonders if you have been playing with fire and it is others who have been burnt.... Liz Freeman for example..."

There was a pause. Kessler nodded again. "You know about that?"

"I found out by chance. It doesn't seem to have been widely publicized. No wonder, it wasn't the fairy tale ending everyone would have hoped for…I went to see her…"

"How is she?"

"It's a bit late for that isn't it?"

Kessler looked away for a moment. "You think me responsible for her…*decline*?"

"I don't know what to think; that is why I am here. Perhaps you could fill in the gaps? I am after all where Liz was this time last year: your *protégé*? Your *natural heir*?"

Even with his sunglasses on Sam could see Kessler rolled his eyes, "That is Farrell's wording and I am sorry for it. Agents are not always mindful of the nurturing proces…"

"Is that what it is? Nurturing? It's not a form of *grooming* then?" Sam saw her opportunity and took it.

Kessler removed his shades, clearly taken aback.

"That's what Liz said to me. She said she felt like she was being groomed. Groomed for *what*? What could she have meant?"

Kessler paused. "What do you know of Liz?"

"Just what I learned speaking to her the other day."

"I must hold my hand up and accept some responsibility as to what happened. I took Liz and transplanted her into what I hoped would be a world of opportunity, but unfortunately it is a world not without its corrupt side. I regret that she became exposed to the worst of it. I also regret I did not anticipate these dangers and safeguard her. I can understand she may hold me responsible but, and excuse me for seeming callous, she had freewill in all this. No gun was held to her head?"

"She became addicted to Cocaine?"

"Yes." Kessler replied, "She had extraordinary talent, I had high hopes for her but she enjoyed, rather too much, the glamour and the social side of what I offered. It became clear she developed a compulsion. I urged her to seek help and to refrain from indulging in the lifestyle she had chosen. Help *was* offered."

Sam sensed the artist's genuine concern.

He repeated his earlier question. "How is Liz?"

"She is getting herself back on track I think." Sam smiled, "She is back with her family."

"Ah, see what I mean about family? She will make great progress in their care...I did help...financially...I fear the family thought it a pay off. I rather think Farrell encouraged their silence in negotiating this. I cannot blame them for thinking badly of me. I made mistakes; I hope you do not think too poorly of me?"

"She doesn't even attempt to paint anymore you know?" Sam said.

"A great shame. Can you imagine losing your desire in such a manner?"

"I can't...but then probably neither could she...it is a very sad story. It could of course been more so, it could have been one with fatal consequence."

Kessler was silent; his hands toyed with the sunglasses he held.

"You asked me my impressions, what are yours?" Sam broke the silence.

Kessler shrugged, sliding his Ray-Bans back on. "I suppose I purposely avoid asking too many questions for fear I disapprove of what I may discover...how is that for an answer?"

"Lacking!" Sam responded.

Kessler laughed, "So, ask me what it is you wish to know?"

"Okay..." Sam thought for a moment, "Dave told me of your *Originators*...the source for your inspiration...the same source that torments Dave in his dreams. Don't you wonder what force is responsible, what motives there may be?"

Kessler took a lengthy pause before answering, and finally, when he did, it was with another question, "Can *you* explain inspiration? Can you put your finger on what makes you want to capture an imagining on canvas? Is the sensation of painting...creating, a *lifeless* experience? Does it not consume you in a way you find impossible to quantify? Are you not possessed by some driving force? You understand this...I know... you *share* this. You are not Liz Freeman. You do not need cocaine to stimulate you...you have your Art....*we* have our Art....*it* is *ou*r compulsion...whatever happens to us, however questioning or challenging...we shall never abandon it..."

Ivory Black

Dave felt the blood rushing to his head; it throbbed with the passage of fluid through its vessels. He felt a tearing stretch through his torso, arms pulled outwards, hands slightly clenched, large iron nails splintering through each palm. He tried to move but in vain, his legs extended upwards, feet secured as his hands. He found himself crucified, nailed to an upturned cross. Dave sensed movement around him; he became aware of an assembled crowd - sneering, chattering, taunting. His eyes tried to focus on the source. He felt hot lashes of liquid scald his skin, igniting on contact, mini fireballs exploding into the acrid air surrounding him. His eyes struggled harder, fighting the pain, seeking understanding of his upturned environment. The crowd became visible: dancing grotesques, dirty misshapen travesties of nature with stumpy limbs all flailing in a chaotic jig, genitals exposed - expelling searing diseased urine, anointing Dave with it; bawdy torturers intent on degradation, whooping and clamouring. From the pit of his stomach Dave formed a scream.

Dave's body convulsed as if a sudden jolt of electricity had charged through his being. He lurched upright, sweat draining from his pores, his chest heaving rapidly like that of an exhausted dog. Sam was awake too, alerted by his sudden movement. She saw the fear in his eyes, the look of anguish and confusion. "It's ok..." she comforted, "Breathe... just breathe." She placed her hands on his chest; he flinched, crying out. Large angry blisters scattered his torso, Sam gasped.

Dave's body trembled, his eyes stared, with his parched mouth barely open, cracked words emerged, "Am I safe? Am I safe?"

Dave sat on the sofa his knees drawn up, clasping the china mug containing tea that had long gone cold. His expression was that of one stunned. He had hardly uttered a word since waking from his nightmare; it was as if part of him had not returned.

Sam held the phone to her ear, one eye remaining on her partner. Fin had seemed the natural person to call. She had an idea and though she knew it carried risks, frankly she had had enough. "It's time to bring in the *big guns* Fin; can you get yourself over here?"

Dorothy *Dot* Wheeler was eighty two. She lived alone in a bungalow, kept a tidy garden, owned a Yorkshire terrier named Dillie and held the august title of Reiki Master. She had taught Sam, it was she who had carried out Sam's attunement, the procedure which aids in the opening and expanding of innate psychic ability. When Sam had talked of *big guns* it was Dorothy to whom she had been referring.

Dave lay on the therapy table in Dorothy's spare room. It was early evening; soft diffused light filled the curtain drawn space. A framed portrait of Christ looked down from one wall, serenity in his eyes. On a fireside shelf sat assorted crystals, in one corner a cross legged Buddha looked on through meditative eyes. Even before any treatment commenced the positivity was tangible.

Dorothy gently arranged pillows beneath Dave's head. Her tiny embroidered oriental slippers padded on the beige carpet as she moved. Her grey hair was piled into an enormous bun that risked defying gravity, her petite frame beneath giving her the appearance of a cotton bud. She gestured to the doorway, Sam and Fin followed her out.

"He is nice and relaxed now," she said, her voice soft with perfectly rounded vowels. "We will give him time to settle." She smiled and ushered her visitors into the lounge. "Poor lamb he's been through so much," Dorothy tentatively touched at her bun, "My Darling I wish you had told me."

Sam sat next to Fin on the busy floral sofa, "It's been hard to know what to make of it all Dot....things have been so crazy."

"I can imagine." Dot turned to Fin, "We are going to have our work cut out in there I fear. Are you up for the task?"

Fin nodded, "I will take your lead...only intervene if at all necessary. I have attended many exorcisms before...and in effect what we are doing is very similar."

"Indeed..." Dot had the bearing of a general being reported to by one of her officers. "Good."

Fin added, "Though in Dave's case possession is not complete? It seems he more likely has some...*parasitic* entity looking for a stronghold to complete dominance?"

"We will know soon enough if that is the case." Dot replied, "I agree that seems likely and therefore we all present must be deeply grounded. Such an opportunist, as this entity *surely* is, will look for any weakness. We shall all be extremely vulnerable to attack unless we take every precaution. I need to firmly warn you both of the danger." Dot's china blue eyes shifted from one of her guests to the other. "So ... let us take some time to prepare ...."

Kessler held his palm against his right eye, testing the vision through its opposite number; the canvas appeared as no more than a tumult of colour. He blinked; darted his eye across the paintings expanse. He switched eyes, left palm to left eye, a chaotic smear of fiery hues the result. He pulled his mobile from the pocket of his denim suit jacket. "Ian Connaught." Kessler spoke into the mouthpiece; the voice dial function saving him peering at his contact list.

"Connaught Law Practice.." came the swift reply."

"Put me through to Ian Connaught please. Tybalt Kessler here; it's a matter of some urgency."

Sam and Fin sat quietly on borrowed dining chairs in each of the far corners of Dot's spare room, the curtained window separating them. Lying on the therapy table, arms at his side dressed in tracksuit bottoms and a t-shirt, Dave breathed softly, eyes closed. Dot stood behind his head, performing a ritual designed to self cleanse. Her moves were slow, deliberate and graceful, her breathing calm. *The calm before the storm.*

Kessler ended the call; he paused, looking as best he could around the studio space, he smiled. He slipped the phone back in his pocket; the expression in his failing eyes was one of resolve.

Sam cast Fin an anxious look.

He smiled mouthing, "Don't worry." He patted the back pack under his chair, its compartment unzipped, allowing him easy access to its stash of blessed water.

Above Dave's head, suspended from the ceiling rose, a mobile of crystals gently clinked and turned. Dot rubbed her palms together as she mouthed an invocative prayer. She began tracing symbols in the air above Dave's head then moved slowly around the couch addressing his body returning finally to where she began.

"Power symbols," Sam whispered, Fin nodding in response.

Dot placed her hands, palms down, about a centimetre distance from Dave's eyes. She inhaled deeply. Dave's back suddenly arched; Dots neck thrust her head upright she exhaled slowly.

The curtains billowed, flailing inwards; Sam shifted in her chair. The crystal mobile chimed louder, a foreign breeze manipulating it. A chill descended, light faded, a creeping rank smell seeped into the air. Dot repositioned her hands, this time on either side of Dave's head; his body flinched, eyes flickering behind closed lids. Sam had a hand to her mouth, her eyes moist. Fin felt goose bumps prickle his forearms, he glanced at his tattoo, closed his eyes momentarily in prayer. A crash came from the wall as the picture of Christ clattered to the floor. Fin jumped in his chair, his eyes snapping open. The curtain ballooned wildly hiding Sam and Fin from each other. Fin grabbed the loose fabric tying it into a large knot, reassuring Sam in the process. Sam rubbed her arms; the room was icy cold now and her breath misted the air. Dot's hands were journeying key points across Dave's body; each adjustment caused a jolt through him. She remained calm, focussed, undaunted. The swirling wind flapped at the sheet beneath Dave, lifting its corners. Its force grew in intensity, now buffeting the slight figure of Dot, the large bun on her head as unyielding as she herself. Her mouth moved, words inaudible, the cyclone noisy, now dislodging all objects in its path. Suddenly Dave's hands hurled up from his sides, grabbing at his own neck. Dots eyes darted toward Fin; he took his cue, leaping from his seat grabbing Dave's hands, wrenching them free, angry welts in their place. Sam cried out; she stood hands at her mouth. An intensely powerful force threw Fin backwards, his back slamming the side wall, delivering him to the floor in a crumpled heap. Sam rushed to him.

He smiled, "I'm ok..." he flexed his neck clicking a subluxated vertebra back into place; Sam helped him to his feet. Their focus returned to Dave. They stood frozen, Fins hand still in Sam's, her grip tightening. The gross heaving figure, a repulsive parody of femininity met their gaze. Straddling Dave its obese bulk mimicking the throws of carnal lust it rocked, its features twisted; a thing of hellish nightmares.

Page 186

Dot seemed unfazed, continuing her incantations ignoring its presence just as one would dismiss an attention seeking child.

Fin pulled Sam to him, sensing her desire to intervene. "Be strong." he whispered, "She's getting to them, be strong for him."

The therapy table rocked from the creatures exaggerated thrusts, its hips slamming and revolving, its pudgy hands caressing Dave's chest; its shrieks ones of paroxysmal excitement. Sam looked on, unable to disguise her disgust, her hand in Fins, grateful for his heat in the freezing room.

"Look through it... not at it," Fin reassured, "it's a distraction Sam, it's an artifice...you've seen *The Wizard of Oz,* right? Remember when you first see the wizard, all booming voice, smoke and flames..?"

"Yeah..." Sam managed a half smile.

"And Toto pulls the curtain away...and it's a little old man pulling levers, working a machine creating what everyone thinks is the wizard?"

Sam laughed through her tears, "Yes. I remember."

"Same thing Sam; It's an illusion. The Devil is a conjurer, full of cheap tricks and deception; he puts on a good show," Fin hugged her, "Look...see what our thoughts have done..." the apparition faded with his words, the table's rocking ceased.

Dot looked across at Sam, "Do you feel up to lending me a hand? I think I may need it." She turned to Fin, "Young man, I want you ready. It's time for us to flush this vile entity out, free this darling boy of its influence; we must close the vibrational doorway through which it came..." Dots eyes were burning, shiny bright like a child's marble, darting from each of her allies to the other. Her demure looks belied the gravity of her words, her tone was sober, her resolution as keen as a razors edge. She placed a hand tenderly on Dave's shoulder, "We must drive the infernal back whence it came. Sam you will work with me, take his right side," Sam moved. "Finlay darling...be ready to assist, the diabolic will no doubt pull every trick from their bag. They will not give up without a considerable fight. They want this boy." She fixed Fin with an earnest gaze, "Do whatever you must young man." She glanced down at Dave, "This mans soul is at stake."

Fin nodded.

Dot took a cleansing breath. "I call upon you Angels... fill me with love and light..." her face softened, her expression sublime she placed her hands above Dave's heart. Sam instinctively followed suit, her hands on the left side of his chest. Dave's body spasmed, his heels and elbows digging into the padding of the table, chest and pelvis arching up. Dot and Sam worked in union, encouraging healing energy to pour through their bodies and out through their fingers. The table quaked, shaking on its legs, the eerie wind whipped up once more battering the two women, Sam's hair lashing at her face, her clothes rippling. A low growl resonated from Dave's chest, his mouth opened, lips dry and cracked.

"No...........no.............NO......... NO........"

The word *No* again and again, building to strangled cries, an agonised look on his face. Inside every fibre of his body tensed, being forced to resist. Sam held fast, continuing her task, focussed and alert, detaching from the distressing sights and sounds. Her thoughts were on the bright, white light of *universal energy*. Dave's protestations changed, to anguished wails. His hands jerked towards his chest pushing the women's hands aside. He tore at his t-shirt neckline, ripping it downwards, revealing his chest shiny with sweat though the room was chilled. He grabbed at his own pectorals, finger nails tearing the flesh in a frenzy of clawing. Fin moved to help, pulling Dave's arms above his head, pinning them back with his body weight. Sam gulped then inhaled, replacing her hands, continuing her task; her eyes met Dot's encouraging gaze. Dot's face now wore a beatific mask, ageless, ethereal; she positively glowed. Sam took courage from the sight and smiled, feeling the self same goodness flow within her. Murmurs chanted, seemingly escaping from behind the walls, frantic backward chants in an unknown tongue, rasping, ranting, voices, escalating in volume. Fin glanced from one wall to the other. Crazed writing started to appear as if scribed by an unseen frantic hand. Scrawls in ancient text, Archaic Latin...dripping red; echoic voices reinforced the written words. The seated Buddha's face appeared to change, a sad cast replacing contentment; from the corners of its rested eyes tears began to shed, droplets of blood falling into its cupped hands resting in its lap. Standing behind the head of the table Fin's hands locked tight around Dave's wrists, stretching the arms in their sockets, using all his will to fight their urge to thrash. Dave's face looked back at him, sneering now; an inhuman expression tainted with hate. He spat at Fin, growling, teeth clenched. At that moment he looked more beast than man. Fin felt the mucus drop in his eye. He blinked to clear it shaking it loose. He looked to Dot then across to Sam; they continued their work diligently. Dot acknowledged Fin, nodding, smiling. The evil was being challenged; it had met its match. Good was driving it out.

Behind Sam the room's tiny open fireplace burst into life, flames twisted in a sinewy dance licking at the surround. Fin saw the inhuman face that peered through the flickering heat, an ancient evil - its mouth open, howling, the emit like the turn of a long rusted screw. The room still wore its chill, though the fire raged fierce in its grate. On either side of Dave, Dot and Sam worked downwards, now at his legs which kicked and splayed. Fin kept him pinned down whilst the women tried as best they could to avoid his thrashing feet. From the self inflicted wounds across Dave's chest blood began to spurt, splashing the faces of those around him. Dot unperturbed, barely blinked, Sam gasped but did not falter, Fin kept his hold.

And there, at the foot of the table the knotted withered creature faded into view. With bony fingers stretched with translucent leathery skin, it clung to Dave's right ankle. Its twisted form held Dave's foot almost in an embrace, as a small child might perversely cling to its favourite blanket. Large jaundiced eyes gazed outwards, blinking, filmy lids slithering across each orb.

The fireplace cleared of flames. The table curtailed its dance. The wind died down. Dave's body calmed. The voices fell silent. The walls lost their unearthly graffiti and the Buddha's tears dried. Silence....stillness.

Fin relaxed his grip on Dave's wrists, returning his arms to his sides. Dot traced a last few symbols in the restored temperature air; Sam took a deep relieved breath.

The creature's knuckles bulged like carbuncles from its clasping grip. It looked...pathetic. Compared to the preceding diabolic siege that had ensued this *thing* was paltry. This was the demonic seed, the parasite that sought dominion of its host. It shiftily gazed at its assembled audience, adjusting its position slightly, a look more desperate than malicious in its eyes.

Fin had returned to the chair in the corner of the room, reached into his backpack and withdrawn a bottle of blessed water from within. Dot began reciting a prayer, her right hand painting her final shape in the air. Fin took the top from the bottle, moved to the foot of the table and raising the bottle high, he poured its contents onto the creature below, its eyes upturned.

A tiny cry emerged hardly audible to the human ear but outside the neighbourhood dogs began to howl.

Dot had recommended that Dave spend the next day resting; he had slept during the car ride home and had gone straight to bed. Sam had stayed awake most of the night, enjoying witnessing Dave's peaceful, deep sleep. She had never seen him so at ease; he was a man unburdened.

The following day Dave had snoozed on and off, eaten very little and spoken few words. The scratches on his chest had faded remarkably fast, leaving only tiny tracks of red, mementoes of the previous day's ordeal. He complained his muscles were sore but other than that he was in good shape. Sam made a conscious effort to pamper him.

Night seemed to fall slowly, Kessler thought. It had been a beautiful clear day; he had enjoyed the sky's hue through the studio's skylight. He grew increasingly more grateful for colour with each passing day as his sight diminished. He had been so moved today that he had set a canvas on his easel and endeavoured to capture the exact shade of blue. He wanted to see it again after the sun went down, while he was still able. He reprimanded himself for never having studied the sky in such a way before. Even a cloudless blue sky is not just one shade, in places mauve dips its toes; in others a powdery lighter blue scatters the vista. How joyful it was to see.

Dave sat in bed watching T.V., a tray Sam had prepared on his lap. The screen showed underwater footage of sharks, winding their way through murky primeval depths; the accompanying voice over belonging to an actor Dave recognised but could not place. He cut through scrambled egg laden toast and forked it into his mouth.

"Sharks partly locate their chosen prey through detection of electromagnetic fields, caused by electrical charges within the prey's cells ... in effect an aura of radiating energy lures the shark ... without knowing it victims signal their presence to these effective and ruthless predators ..."

The sky light finally filled with the majesty of night. Kessler smiled; the blue staring from his canvas a trace of things past. It made little difference now whether he wore his

Page 191

spectacles or not; he tossed them onto the cluttered workbench beside him. He unscrewed a large container of turpentine and poured some into a jam jar, returning the container near the workbench's edge. The rags beside it sat stained and crumpled, witnesses to the subtleties of shades to which the canvas now comprised. He reached for his packet of *More*, lighting one in his mouth, taking a long slow draw...

A shadow passed overhead.

Kessler agitated the brush; the jam jar's fluid contents becoming a mini ocean of blue. Stretching for a fresh rag and misjudging its distance his elbow caught the container of turps, its contents quickly flooding the surface of the workbench on which it stood.

Above, the vast skylight shattered with a thunderous crash, shards of glass raining down, a hail of showering jagged splinters cascading into the studio below. A piercing screech accompanied the creatures swooping form, its fibrous wings flapping, slowing its descent to the floor. Kessler's antique easel toppled, taking the artist with it - crashing into the workbench beside him. The long slender cigarette tumbled from his lips, instantly igniting the chemical soaked puddle of soiled rags strewn across the surface. He howled as the burst of sudden flames charred his face. Stumbling he hauled himself to his feet and with hands alight he patted and slapped at his jacket, desperate to dampen the lashing flames. He tottered backwards on his heels, eyes flashing, pulling on what sight he had to view the object of destruction before him.

And there it stood, with wings slightly apart, hot breathed; its cloven feet shifting its weight. *The Soul Feaster*.

Irridescent White

Dave had wearied of being cooped up inside; this morning had seen another bright sky herald it. He had slipped out of bed leaving Sam to a well deserved lie-in, pulled on a pair of shorts, a t-shirt and his trainers and now jogged his old familiar route. Today though it felt different; he felt different…difficult to put a finger on exactly how, and in any case his brain was not ready for complex thought. A jog was the medicine he craved: fresh clean air, the only demand one of keeping his feet moving. Thoughts came and went but without analysis; mindfulness. Truth be told he remembered little of the last few days; the weeks before that were foggy at best. Today though he felt happy and that was quite enough.

Bleary eyed, Sam shuffled to the kitchen, clicking the T.V. on en-route. She had been surprised to roll over and find an empty space beside her, a yellow post-it replacing Dave's warm body, *gone jogging* its message. A good sign she had consoled herself, perhaps today he would start to speak more? Dot had said to be patient. There would be *a period of readjustment*. He had probably carried that *demon seed* since his parents' deaths; part of who he thought he was had vanished with it. Sam shuddered to think of it. What would remain? She fired up the kettle, aware of the of the T.V. news reporter's voice, but paying little attention, until she heard the name *Tybalt Kessler* and that there had been a fire.

When Dave arrived back home Sam was on the sofa facing the TV; a mug of Earl Grey tea in her clasped hands. Unusual to see her still in her bathrobe, he thought; ordinarily she beat him to the shower. She waved for him to join her, pointing at the screen.

The rolling news channel had stuck with the Kessler story, regurgitating the same scant facts every few minutes, promising updates: Early morning footage of the studio warehouse engulfed by flames, deployed fire crews, then cut to a live report from outside the smoking remains, press jostling for position, emergency services trying to exercise their duties, a glum reporter standing centre stage.

"It is now assumed that renowned artist Tybalt Kessler perished in the fire that took hold earlier this morning at his studio here in Old Portsmouth. Controversy followed the artist's life. Now with confirmed reports the artist was here painting when the fire broke out and it being unlikely he could survive the inferno that quickly ensued, it seems his colourful reputation and talk of a curse surrounding him will only be enhanced by his premature death. Tributes are already beginning to come in...."

Sam lowered the volume; Dave was sat beside her, eyes scanning the scene listening intently.

"I'll get you a tea..." Sam rose and pecked Dave on the forehead. His eyes stared ahead. She kept her eyes on him as she crossed to the kitchen space, passing her painting of Kessler's chateau on its easel. Dave sat motionless saying nothing. Sam unplugged the mobile phone that was charging on the counter, glancing at the handset. "You've got some missed calls... must've come when I was sleeping in... Steele, oh Professor Naismith....Fin, and an unrecognised number. You feel up to listening to voice mails?"

Dave was still silent. Sam poured some tea bringing his phone with it back to the sofa.

"You listen to them love," Dave answered, a delayed response to her question.

Sam put the phone to her ear: D.C.S Steele's message was brief, information on the studio fire, reassuring Dave he could take some overdue leave. Naismith was a bag of nerves; obviously he had caught the early news wanting to know if the rumours were true. Fin on the other hand sounded calm and unsurprised, more interested in Dave's wellbeing than Kessler's fate. Sam listened to the final message, caller unknown.

"Hello. This is Ian Connaught. I am a solicitor

representing Tybalt Kessler. 1 have been instructed by my client to order a courier to deliver some papers to you. On receipt could you call me please?"

Sam looked back at the television screen. The news report started its loop again: A photograph of Kessler, shots of the fire, the glum faced reporter... she turned to Dave, "It seems we're getting some papers from Kessler."

Dave met her eyes, *"Papers?"*

Burnt Sienna

Autumn; The Dordogne, France. Pierre Laroche drove his four by four through the magnificent castle gates, flanked by the original fortified walls that had stood since the fifteenth century. The beautifully restored chateau stood some way in the distance. Laroche took the winding side road through the grounds of the sixteen hectare vineyard. As Chef des Vignes he occupied the three bedroomed winemakers cottage discretely out of view. The tyres gently rolled to a stop. Laroche quickly leapt from the driver's seat and headed to the passenger side, he opened the door as widely as it allowed and offered his hand. The passenger's own badly scarred hand passed him a sturdy walking cane which he took, leaning it against the front wheel arch. The passenger shuffled forward in his seat, Laroche helping. Laroche gave the man back his cane and linked arms with him, guiding him to the cottage front door. The walk was slow. Laroche's guest wore a large straw sun hat,, not unlike a Stetson, dark glasses shielded his eyes, his thick beard of stubble was three quarters white where only months ago it had shown only a hint of age. What remained visible of his face, like his hands was badly scarred, a lasting souvenir of the fire that had almost claimed his life.

Laroche spoke kindly in broken English, "I have made great alterations inside, you will be...comfortable here I know."

"You have been a dear friend," the burned man replied, "A true and loyal friend. No man is luckier than I."

"Monsieur Kessler it is I who is lucky, you have always been so good to me... working for you, it has been my joy."

Kessler laughed, "Ah well, now you work for me no more. I am reliant on *you* now my friend. How fortunes reverse."

"We shall want for nothing," Laroche answered, gesturing toward the many vines, "we shall surely not go

Page 196

thirsty here!"

The two men laughed.

"And what of your new employers?" Kessler asked, "How do you find them?"

"Most kind. Lively! A good choice... they know little of wine but they will learn. Oh how you would love the Mademoiselle's paintings...." Laroche paused, "Please forgive me..."

Kessler brushed the remark aside, "Do not worry my friend. Though my eyes can barely see... I am not sad. I have seen things few others have *dreamed* of. And now...I must find *other* pursuits, no? This for me is a new chapter; do not feel pity for me."

Laroche opened the door to the cottage, "Come Monsieur, I have someone here most eager to meet you!"

"Oh?"

"Yes, yes..." Laroche answered, "Meet *Boto*."

Kessler felt himself lead to an armchair in which he sat.

Laroche disappeared from the room briefly talking animatedly. Kessler heard an excited bark and a patter of clawed feet and then felt a nuzzling at him and a licking of his face. He reached for the source of all this attention, his hands stroking the soft straw coloured coat of the young dog before him. The dog licked again at his face as he leaned forward. "Hello Boto....." Kessler rubbed at the dog's neck.

"He will be your eyes!" Laroche announced, watching the affectionate greeting taking place.

Kessler smiled; his hand running through the animal's fur.

"See..." Laroche observed, "You are friends already. That is good."

"Yes..." Kessler answered, tears flooding from his blind eyes... "Hello boy, hello Boto."

Page 197

Kessler's Letter

On your receipt of this missive one must assume events have taken an irreversible turn towards the final.

I have requested that my Solicitor Connaught be rapid in following my instruction and to ease its completion with discretion. It is my hope he complies.

The chateau is yours. I hope you love it as I do; the vineyard too. The employees are loyal, more family than staff. I am confident they will smooth your transition.

As for my Art and any legacy it should bring, I urge you to continue what my Foundation has begun. I sense you will share the deep joy that arises from its work.

On a personal note I ask you judge me not too harshly in all that has occurred. With deeper knowledge of the Foundation and its life affirming work I trust you will see the balance struck.

I am not without blame. I am sure you wonder what role I have had to play in all that has unfolded. In truth not even I fully know. I know great Art compels man, I suspect through its powerful forces it reaches his soul. Art amplifies, intensifies what lives in the mind and what lies in the heart. Art is indeed powerful and power may enable or corrupt a man - it is his choice and his alone that determines the outcome. It was Carl Jung who said, *If our civilisation were to perish it would be due more to stupidity than evil.*

Free will is a wonderful thing. We all within us carry such potential. Look within - David and Sam; live up to yours.

Tybalt Kessler.

Printed in Great Britain
by Amazon.co.uk, Ltd.,
Marston Gate.